The Song of Forgetfulness
Book One

# Whisper Gatherers

by

Nicola McDonagh
http://www.thesongofforgetfulness.com

## Books in The Song of Forgetfulness series

*This book is a work of fiction. Names, characters, places and events portrayed are either products of the author's imagination or are used fictitiously. Any character resemblance to actual persons living or dead is entirely co-incidental.*

*No part of this work may be reproduced or transmitted in any form or by any means, electronic or mechanical without written permission from the author.*

Copyright © 2015 Nicola McDonagh
All rights reserved.

ISBN: 1514316080

ISBN-13: 978-1514316085

Cover design by Daphne deMuir
Original photographs by Nicola McDonagh

*To Martin for all his help, support and patience with me. I couldn't have done it without you.*

## Chapter One
*Too High*

Sweat trickled down my armpits and back as I shinnied upwards. The climb was harder than it looked. I stopped midway and clung onto the thick twine for a much needed breather. The air hovered still for a sec and in that quiet I swear I heard an owlet hoot. Or maybe it was the ghosties of our lost ones wipple-warbling through the dirt-free walkways of Cityplace. Nah, what rot. Anyhoo, best not pause my ascent to ponder such a notion. It was nearly dusk-to-dawn time and my outsideness was in jeopardy.

"Flimsyfem. Feeblewomb," nasty voices beneath my swinging feet heckled each clammy-fingered fumble that I made. If I'd been on ground level they'd be red-nosed crying like a bub, but I was not, so I ignored their goading and carried on.

I quickly pulled myself up the rope. Too vigorously as it turned out. The cord began to sway causing my shoulder to bump into the side of the massive metal frame. Although it hurt, I did not cry out. Even when the heat from the humming gastubes scorched my ear and I smelt the burnt sugar stench of singed hair. I kept shutums. If not, the bet would be lost.

Shaking my head to dispel the sizzle-sting, I over handed bit by bit until I reached the middle support rung. As I scrambled onto the narrow ledge, I heard a familiar two-pitch whistle. Flashlighters. Nad. I couldn't be caught again.

The last time they fingered me sneak-thieving inside the Minion quarters outside Central Local. Well, my bro dared me to go and ask one of the dark-eyed dwellers exactly what the huff they did. Never did get to find out, though. All I managed to do was to scare a grubby-faced little 'un when I held out my mutant mitts. A thing I do too often as it turns out. Like accepting dares. Although this one was by far the least hazardous, despite it being so high up. One day I would say no to these challenges. Yeah, right.

"Flimsyfem!"

"Feeblewomb!"

Yep, I know, I know. Derisive calls did not help to clamp down my fear at teetering on the edge of an info board beam. Although nervous and height-stricken, I looked below to where Drysi and Hrypa slouched. "Oy, tug on the end of the rope so that I can slip-slide down before the Longarms get a whiff of wrong doing."

The over washed sissy-necked juves fled. I was left to hide as best I could before the ever vigilant Cityguards came searching for Curfewcrashers. Always get more folk risking being nabbed when something oddly occurs. The under-breath murmurs about the Carnies, and the kiddles that disappeared had residents all skittish with the need to know info that was not forthcoming.

Once, when these flesh-gobblers and their notsofunfair came to these parts, the mayor had to call in the S.A.N.T.S. to bumrush them out before they hoodwinked us and filched all the grain. Some say they use it to lure the birdybirds so they can suck out their eyes and brains.

A recollection stirred in my noggin. A half-memory of something best forgotten. Ah, Carnieval. That was it. I shuddered at the memory of their hideous show then sidestepped my way behind the vidscreen into almost darkness.

I put my hand on a cross section support strut and felt something gunky. I lifted my fingers to my face. It took a while for my eyes to become accustomed to the gloom, but they did. What was stuck there made me hold my breath as I glanced along the metal pole.

Wow and then some. They'd been here. Birdles. The white plops spattered along the beam proved it. Not that I'm an expert or anything, but the size and shape of said bowel squirts would indicate a sphincter no bigger than a newbies fingernail. No hominid I knew had a backside that small. Besides I found it hard to believe that any Citydweller would climb the central vidscreen to do a dump.

"Adara."

Huffin' hell and back. Santy Breanna's voice crashed through the buzzing of the neolights. I almost lost my balance. With a gulp, I inched sideways along the ridge and peeked down at the plaza. Big mistake. The antivertigo tabs I'd taken earlier had worn off. I'd come over with a severe case of the wobbles.

"Adara, you are too much of an age to be playing 'gohideandseek'. I'll not count to a specified number in the hope that you'll appear. No, I'll just stand right here and wait." Santy put her hands on her hips and lifted her head. I slid behind the screen and stood motionless.

A low bonging sound resonated around

the square. I closed my eyes. Curfew chimes. I had no desire to be caught by the Flashlighters and spend the night in the filthhole, but the tone in Santy's voice made me stay where I was. Every time she used my full name I knew I was in trouble. I moved my head round the corner, watched her pull back her shoulder length strawberry blonde hair and twist it into a tight knot.

"Hear that? You'd better come out right now before the Longarms appear. The Sheriff doesn't look kindly upon re-offenders."

Her words activated two hand-in-hand, lip locked 'dults who sat on the rim of the palm tree-shaped fountain opposite the infoboard. They stood 'bruptly, dropped their hands and skedaddled in different directions as shiftily as a Minion caught nattering with a Highup. I thought Santy would scarper too, what with the lateness of things, but she remained, arms folded, foot tapping, serious of face.

Inhaling deeply, I prepared to wait it out. Moontime was fast approaching and with it, danger of exposure.

I squinted when the bright spiral security beacons blasted on, floodlighting the entire space. I'd never seen the square like that before, never from such a height.

The large paved rectangle that made up most of the plaza was dull in the extreme, and the fountain plonked in the middle did nowt to enhance its gloomy look. Up here it took on a more eerie appearance. Smothered in a sickly yellow glow, it made the surrounding concrete buildings look as if they were about to throw up. I thought I was too and stretched my neck out to see what Santy was up to so that I could make my descent.

I happened to look towards the perimeter fence, although far in the distance I thought I saw a blip of white light just behind it. I narrowed my eyes and made out the shivering shape of a hominid crouching.

"Right, that's it. Time is up and I am gone. You can wait for punishment." Santy gave a brief eyescan of the square, turned away from the infoboard and strode towards Cityhall.

I reluctantly yanked my gaze away from the suspish figure. Despitebeing all a-feared, I quickly grappled my way down, unhooked the zip rope, bundled it into my pants pocket and tiptoed up behind her back.

"Hi, hi, Santy. Shouldn't you be indoors? Curfew's chimed."

She swivelled round grabbed my right ear and dragged me past Cityhall, the fountain, the Seedbank Centre and through the arched gateway towards the folkdwellings. I placed my hand over hers in an attempt to ease the pressure her fingers made on my lobe, but she was clamped on tight.

"You're lucky the Curfewkeepers are late, or we'd be shivering in the dirt pit till sunup. You want us to go to the Decontamination House? Or thrown out into the Wilderness to be eaten by Wolfies, or worse, Carnies?"

I said nowt except for, "Ow," then mused briefly on what she'd said. Just the thought of those low-grade carnivores made my gut flip and my hands moisten.

Santy did not let go of my lobe, which throbbed, until we reached Puritytowers. I rubbed my burning flesh. Santy shook her head. "That was a close call. Next time, and don't look at me as if there won't be, I'll leave you out there to fend for yourself. I thought you'd outgrown these bub-like shenanigans."

"But, they called me a flimseyfem."

"So? Adara, you are nearing the time for joining. You must be 'dult now and take on the role of legal age."

With a sigh, I lifted my head. I never tired

of looking up at the building we lived in. Even by Cityplace standards, this was an impressive structure. As tall as any mythical oak, Puritytowers loomed over the rest of the abodes like a giant many-sided mirror. The reflective outer cladding sparkled in the daylight and became a black mysterious object at night. When I was a bub, I used to think it was alive.

I stared at the roof, at the long slim metal pole that pointed to the sky, and remembered Santy Breanna tell me that it was a lightning rod to protect the building from being split in two during a storm. To this day, I flinch each time I hear thunder.

There came an unfamiliar rustling from behind the building. Followed by a murmur, guttural and low. Then, a thin grey mist appeared. It spread out and fingered its way towards us.

"Inside before they lock up for the night."

"But, Santy, that noise, that fog."

"In!"

She pushed me forward and I almost fell through the entrance portal.

"Now, up those stairs, let me time you."

I bolted up the polished steps and flung open the great glass doors. The white hallway was brightly lit. I was dazzled each time I set foot in the space. The familiar smell of just-washed everything stung my nostrils till I sneezed.

"I believe you must be the only hominid in NotSoGreatBritAlbion to react so allergy wise to clean."

My nose ran. However, before I could commit the transgression of wiping it on my sleeve, Santy Breanna whipped out a nasalwipe from her tunic pocket and pressed it against my snout. "Ta." I was about to drop the soiled thing onto the floor, when she raised her eyes to the wallcams. "Oh, right, yep, sorry. Habit." I threw the snotty sheet into the wall incinerator and winked at whoever manned the cams.

"Indeed. Just where did you learn such a filthy custom?"

"Erm, well, from you actually."

"What? I have never..." Santy did not finish her sentence. Instead, she gave me a grin. "That was a one-off girly."

"Yeah right."

"Besides, we were out in the Wilderness where toiletries are not readily to hand."

"Erm? As I recall, the only time we went near to the Wilderness, it was only a footstep over the perimeter fence."

"True. I meant Cityparc."

"Cityparc? How can two half dead trees and a patchly-patch of browning grass become a wilderness?"

"It can when it is used for reconnaissance training. No more backchat girly. Go on, up the steps. I shall be clocking your ascent. Yesterday you were two secs slower."

I ran to the great stone staircase at the end of the hallway, waited for Santy Breanna to click on her wrist timer, then legged it up the six flights to our living space.

Nad!

She was already by the front door waiting for me, without a loss of breath.

"Better than yesterday, but still one sec down on your best."

"How do you do that?"

"Outside emergency exit stairs. Plus, I am S.A.N.T. and Backpacker trained."

I let out a whistle through my clenched teeth and bent over to suck in oxy. When I recovered, Santy swiped the unlockcard across the entrance slit and the door opened. A blast of sanitising vapour doused us soundly when we stepped inside.

I sneezed again but avoided smearing the mucus on my clothing. Instead, I reached over to the hankybank attached halfway down the wall, pulled out a cloth, wiped my noz and disposed of the thing in the Sanitybin next to it. It made a gurgling noise as if swallowing, then all went quiet. When I was no taller than knee height, I thought a Wolfie lived in the refuse tube and guzzled down all our rubbish whole. Santy stared at me. I felt a prickly heat rise up my face.

"Addy, I noticed an unusual stain upon your pantaloons. Now, the only place that I can think of that would produce such a smear is the wastebin site in the Minion quarters, or the Trashland area. I hope you and your chums have not been frolicking in an outlawed place? If any folk eyeballed you and then told, you would be up before the Lawenforcer again."

"No, no, I swear to the OneGreatProvider I was not there."

"Tell the truth."

"I am."

"Then where did you spring from?"

I tried to avoid her unblinking stare, but such was the force of her half-closed eye missile, that I crumpled and blabbed all.

"Drysi and Hrypa dared me to climb the main infoboard in Centralplaza place. They wanted me to tell them if I could see over the perimeter fence for the Carnieval. We thought we heard the thumps and sing-song of said festivities from afar." Santy cast her eyes down and let out a longly sigh. "They said that if I didn't, then they would put it about that I was a feeblefem, scardybird and no S.A.N.T. camp would let me in."

Santy Breanna looked down her long thin nose. "What age are you?"

"Wa? You don't know?"

"I repeat, what age are you?"

"Well, since you have forgot, I shall tell, seventeen orbits and seven moon cycles."

"No more than a bub's breath away from wombreadiness. You should be preparing for a match of settledown, not engaging in kiddle sport."

The mention of my readiness for femhood and bub bearing caused a clenching of my fingers. "I will not become a missus to spend the rest of my lifespan spreadlegged and docile."

"So, you want to be a S.A.N.T.?"

"Yep and then some."

"Then behave as one who would deserve such a special honour and conduct yourself accordingly. Plus, you should respect the memory of your nearest and dearest by behaving in a manner they would be proud of."

I managed to force out a, "Sorry," at the

mention of my departed ma and pa. Santy lost the look of disapproval.

"Quite an achievement. That screen is mighty tall. I think you might have what it takes to step into my shoes."

I grinned and she cuffed me gently on the noggin. We walked through the bright, white hallway into the kinsfolk room where Deogol sat in the same place as I left him at sunrise.

When Santy called his name, he merely tilted his head, grunted, then went back to tip tapping on the keypad. All the while staring into the flickering compscreen as though it held the answer to everything. Santy shook her head and gave forth a greatly sigh. "I wonder your eyes don't melt with all that peering at numbers, symbols and the like. I'll take you both on a camping trip. Some outside air is what you need young male."

Deogol paused from his tapping. "I have no relish for outdoor pursuits. I would have you cease from trying to make me what I am not."

"No good will come from being stuck to the whispering and whirling of those tech things. They are for info only and not meant to be adjusted for your own pursuits. If the sheriff were to…"

My bro lifted his fingers from the keyboard and stood facing Santy Breanna. "I will never be sanitised again. I will commit the worst-of-all-sins before I would let them drag me to the Decontamination place." His face was redder than a bub's in full squeal. Both Santy and I took a step back. Deogol ran his hands through his thick blond hair. "I have found things out. Things that the great infoboard does not tell. Things about the Agros and the missing Kiddles."

## Chapter Two
*Giving In To Temptation*

Santy shut the comp lid and pushed it to the back of the glass-topped desk. Deogol frowned but said nowt. I winked at my bro. My belly gave out a roar and I rubbed it. "Not taken in any nutri since morningmeal. I am greatly famished.

"Not surprised what with all your doings high up."

"Addy, did you do the dare?"

"I did."

Deogol stood and gave me his fist to bump. Santy raised her eyebrows for a sec, then went to the foodprep room that directly led on. I waited until I heard her open cupboards and rattle plates around, before beckoning Deogol to sit on the comfycouch next to me. What with all the ear pulling and sniffles, I had all but forgot about my excellent discovery so was eager to tell my bro.

"I saw something."

"What?"

"Birdypoop."

"Where?"

"On the ledge behind the great vidscreen

in Centralplaza."

My bro gave me a look of intense. "You can't tell anyone."

"Can't tell anyone what?" Santy stood in the doorframe and folded her arms.

"Erm."

"Adara, tell or you'll not have any soylygrub this eve."

My tum screamed at me to tell, but my nonce and heart would have me keep silent. She gave me another lowered lid look. I gulped and put my hands on my stomach to deaden the loud rumblings that issued from it.

"Well?" Santy looked from me to Deogol then turned her head in the direction of where the smell of heating food came from. "If you do not relinquish the info I have asked for, not only you but your brother, will go without."

"Wha? But that's not fair."

"Perhaps it is not in your eyes Deogol, but I seek honesty in this abode. Anything less is a slight upon our kinship. The info you give will not go further than this place, you know that."

I was humbled by her words and guilt-ridden about Deogol missing a meal. The portions of grub had been somewhat less of late. When I played quickgrab with my bro yesterday I was able to wrap my fingers all the way around his bony wrist. I took in a deeply breath and said, "I found birdyplop behind the great vidscreen in Centralplaza."

Santy put her hand to her mouth. "You must tell no one else. Promise?" I nodded.

"You too Deogol."

"I'll not say a word."

My palms began to sweat a bit at the realisation that I came so close to letting rip when I was above ground. The sight of birdle poop had awakened my birth power. All I craved was to exercise my voice to see if I could bring down a real live birdybird. My inner turmoil must have showed without, as Santy sucked in her cheeks and half closed her eyes. "Adara, you must not take it into your nonce to practise your namegift."

"I wasn't, well, mebbe a bit."

"You must not."

My innards scrunched. My entire time upon this forsaken land was all about deceit and furtive. I had a gift, given to me by who-knows-what, but still, I had it and yearned to use it. "But how will I learn to control it."

"You will not, because I forbid you to try it out. Too much danger is attached to it.

What I say is for the utmost best, of that you can be sure."

"I'll be discreet."

Santy folded her arms and gave me a half smile.

"I promise. It will be as if I never made a sound, so careful."

"Like the last time when you sneaked to the perimeter, bringing forth raptors instead of tweeties?"

"I learned from that Bro, I learned."

"There will be no goings to anywhere by the border fences for either of you. Carnies are rumoured to arrive. Also, Praisebees have been seen trying to get in."

"Praisebees? What do those zealots want in this sanitised setting?

"Who knows? Maybe the Agros have cut back their supplies and they seek comfort here."

"Or mebbe, mebbe they've heard about the Carnieval. They have come to see what those freaks deliver in their bizarro show. Or, mebbe, they want to know what meat tastes like and have heard about Adara and her skill. Mebbe you should sing after all to help ease their sufferings."

"You would ask your sis to reveal herself, become a slave to all who would abuse her gift? Just to satisfy the curiosity of unstable devotees. Or to appease the perverse hunger of Carnies? Those folk are nothing but trouble."

"Some say they cannot help themselves and have gone nutso from the torment of their urges."

"Carnies, mad? My robust behind. They are not afflicted, merely lustful for that which they cannot, should not have." Santy rarely raised her voice and when she did, we knew not to answer back. "All settled?" We both affirmed with a head nod. "Good, now let us go to the foodprep room to partake of our nightly meal."

We followed her to the place and sat down at the round metal table. Santy ladled out a spoonful of soymix. I waited for her to garnish the plate with some greenery like she always did. She did not, instead she sat down and said, "Eat up before it cools. Although tasty enough, I fear this particular flavour is lacking in agreeableness on the palate."

Her portion was less than ours. I began to wonder just how many provisions the Agros were holding back from Cityplace.

We demolished the bland foodstuff. The ache in my innards relented a tad when she poured us some milk as a compensational treat. We gulped it down like a hungry kittle. She watched us drink and I swear I saw a tear form in her left eye. She coughed, picked up the plates and put them in the dishwash. It made a whoosh sound for a sec, then Santy sprayed the table, chairs, heatinghob and walls with hygenespray. Blinking, I pinched my nostrils together so that I wouldn't sneeze, so letting loose more germs. Then sighed and took to staring at my bro.

His eyes were closed, his brow furrowed. He intertwined his fingers before placing them beneath his chin, like someone deep in thought. On looking at him in such a contemplative state, I would have taken him for a wise oldie. I held my breath and thought I would use some telempathy to mind connect in order to find out what the huff he was thinking about. Then I recalled his cryptic words about knowing stuff about the Agros, and my heart stuttered.

"Addy, tomorrow is your last time at the place of learning," Santy said, thus breaking the spell between my bro and I. He opened his eyes and sat back, whilst I slumped a little from the effort of trying to delve inside his noggin. "We must plead your case before the Oldies, see if they will allow you to train as a S.A.N.T."

"I hope they will."

My bro smirked and leant forward. "Yeah, they'll let you go, Addy. Easier than trying to find someone who'd want to be your hubbie. You're too squat, too thick of waist to attract a potential mate. Not in all your juve time has a rutting male come sniffing at this door."

I pinched Deogol's arm most savagely, and he let forth a high-pitched squeal. "I could have the pick of any in Cityplace if I chose. But I do not."

"Well said, Adara. Deogol, those words were not apt. Your sis is of a rotund physique, which may indeed prove unsupportive if she wished to attract one of the opposite. But she has made clear on more than one occasion, she would rather become a Backpacker than a missus."

Deogol sneered.

I blinked slow to indicate I was not fussed by what he'd said. Although a part of me did flinch when he pointed out my huge lack of teensap attention. The othergirlygigs I knew had romfriends in abundance. I became all face pink and hung my head. Santy touched my short cut hair and said, "You have more to offer this sad land than any flighty fem. You will be a most welcome addition to the S.A.N.T. clan."

"If they let me join."

"How can they not? You've been training since a tot. Don't concern yourself about their decision. Now, both of you to bed. Sleep without upset."

We rose and bid each other goodnight, then went to our individual layingdown place. My room was a tad bigger than my bro's, with a window that opened. A prize for showing my deftness at staying clear of said portal when ajar. He, when tested, as are we all when we reach the height of danger, raced straight to it. Santy had to grab his shirt and yank him back to safety before he jumped through. My beddie place was much brighter too. He preferred low-lit accommodation without decoration. I had laser etchings of extinct animals. Kittles and dowgie pics filled the wall above where my beddie stood.

With a touch of my fingers, the images changed. Now, instead of a kittle-cat playing with a length of fibre, my peepholes were gratified with more once-lived creatures that I am told roamed freely around this sadly land of ours. Horsies, deeries, hephalumps and the like, all gone now taken by the long ago plague. I pressed my palm against the image of a pink piggle. It transformed into my favourite long-dead beast, a squiggle. I stroked its tufty ears, its bushyly tail and wished such creatures still abided in this barren place.

My musings ended with a yawn. I turned and opened the door opposite that led into the steamshower. I slap-shoed in, undressed, threw my soiled garments through the flap of the washhole next to the poop bowl, and stepped into the glass-encased cubical. I pressed the eye level button on the wall. The hot vapour rid me of all the dirt I had attracted from my escapade. Despite the soothing nature of the cleansing, and Santy's encouraging words, I could not forget about the birdyplop and felt a pull inside my throat.

With a belly cough, to rid myself of the longing to call to them, I pressed the button to cease the hotly water then stepped out of the shower. After drying myself, I put on a lightweight all-in-one jammie suit I took from the metal talldrawer. It was my favourite bedware. The colour of a winter's sky with spots of white dappled all over it. It reminded me of a snowshower and the fun

Deogol and I had playing splatball when we were small. I yawned, went back into the sleep part of the room, clapped my hands and the lights dimmed. I stretched, yawned again before flopping onto the soft cosiness of the bed. I wriggled under the sheets, lay my head on the supersoft allergysafe pillow and let my lids drop over my weary eyes.

The image of great flocks of birdybirds filled my head. In my make believe musings these birdles landed and pecked on the ground. A thing they have not done since the famine made folk consume everything that still lived. I blinked and rubbed my eyes to dispel the entrancing pic, but when I closed them again, the birdies came back. I tried to think of other things, but nothing could rid me of the flapping creatures.

I rolled onto my belly and pressed my forehead deep into the pillow. After a few secs of shallow breathing, I made up my mind. Although Santy forbade me to sing, my body and brain told me otherwise. I felt a stirring of vocal muscles in my throat. Gagging, I tried to hack out the yearning with chesty hem-hems, but the throbbing ache continued.

Spinning onto my back, I clutched at my neck, sucked in my lips to try not to let out my voice. But I could not. I threw back the coverlings and got out of bed. Walking slowly as if I were a night-walker. I went to the window and opened it. A cool breeze swept across my face. I smelled a faint scent of something sweet and cloying. My nose twitched and my windpipe covering trembled as I sucked in air. I leant out, widened my gob, then let my voice ring out.

## Chapter Three
*The Haunting Of Cityplace*

The sound that came from my mouth was strange. I'd never heard myself sing in such a fashion, and did not know where the long, high notes came from. All I knew was that it felt goodly and right to be calling to the birdybirds. Although, the only feathered creatures that would be around at moontime, would be owlets. My heart near stopped at the thought that I may get the chance to actually see one.

Oh, I'd earholed more than one hooting and screeching, but I could not put a name to the brittle song. When I called to Santy Breanna to witness the noise, she said it was that of a blarnyowl. Then she showed me pics of them on my slab. Their round, flat white faces and big black eyes gave me the heebies. I thought they looked like ghosties. Santy said that some folk believed said Tytonidae were the voices of the dead trying to deliver messages to those that remained. On hearing their jarring peeps, I could not say for sure that she was wrong.

I ached to hear them, so cried out again and closed my eyes. In the blackness behind my lowered lids, flashes of light danced and fell in intricate patterns, until I could almost see a parade of silhouetted creatures. They were nothing like the real beasts they'd shown us from the long gone bygone days in yesteryear class. I found it sadder than sad when watching the vids, that all but the flying animals on the land were extinct. Except for Wolfies. The snarling, hideous beasties that some say roam the Wilderness. I shuddered, glad that I lived in such a secure setting.

Yet, part of me wished to go forth into that savage land and experience its fearsomeness first hand. Since that was not going to happen any time soon, I concentrated my wistfulness on bringing forth a hoolet or two, and sang once more. All remained quiet despite my earnest calling. So I tried again, waited for a response, when none came, I ceased my futile singsong.

I should have gone to beddybyes, but there was something brewing on the wind that whooshed past my face. Troubled, I lifted my head to the sky in search of stars, but there was too much light from the other buildings and the many infoboards that faced each living quarter, for the flickering orbs to be visible. I wished it could be really dark here so that I could see them.

Once, Santy had taken Deogol and me to the edge of Cityplace, right on the border to the Wilderness where the Woodsfolk dwell. She said something secret to the guard and he let us step a few bits into the tree-dense area. We stopped just in sight of the bordercheckpoint. Raising our heads, we stared at the black heavens.

Dots of twinkling light sparkled before our eyes. I was overcome with wonderment at what I gazed upon. On tiptoe, hands outstretched as if to touch them, I stretched my bod upwards. Santy laughed and told me they were too far away. I tried to say I wasn't actually attempting to place my mitt upon a thing beyond our planet, but she had done listening. Scolded me again for being daft. I sulked all the way back home.

Then I heard them.

The shrieking shrill hoots of owlets. The sound drifted past my window, but I saw no birdle. I shuddered as the squeals became louder then faded away.

There was a tip-tapping on my door and I quickly pulled in my head.

"Addy? Are you asleep?"

Closing the window without making a sound, I slipped back between the sheets.

"Addy?"

"Yeah, what?" I said, in as sleepy a manner as I could.

Santy Breanna entered. I made a fake yawn to fool her into thinking that I had been in slumberland. "Did that weird noise not awaken you?"

"Erm, what weird noise?"

"The one that sounded like owlets."

"Owlets? No, can't say that I did. Must have been asleep."

"Really? It was more than quite loud. I would have said if I didn't know any better, that the thing was perched upon your windowsill."

"Shame I missed it then."

"Shame indeed." She walked over and sat on the edge of my bed. "I will ask you once and once only. I hope the answer you give will be honest true. If not, I will be deeply offended. Do you glean my meaning?" I nodded. "Did you let loose your voice for one and all to hear?"

I paused before responding. Hoping that the gap between speaking and thinking of what to say would prove fruitful. I came up with nowt but, "I couldn't help myself. What with finding the birdypoop, thrilling at the thought of becoming a S.A.N.T. I felt impelled to let rip before I choked with yearn."

Santy closed her eyes for a sec then took my hands in hers. She turned them over so that my palms faced the ceiling and counted all of my six fingers. "You have enough strange about you to cause folk to gawk without attracting more attention. I understand more than you realise. I know just how strong an urge it is to fulfil your namegift. But Addy, in your case it would be dangerous in the extreme. I will say again, you must not use your voice, ever."

My nostrils flared for a sec, then I squeezed her hand most fondly. She gave another huge sigh, let go my massive mitts and said, "This I will tell you. Things are becoming out of sorts. A storm most metaphorical approaches. We must prepare to get severely wet."

"Metaphorically?"

"Yep."

"So, not Carnies and their fright-show?"

"No."

"Oh. I glean your meaning Santy, I think, and will behave." She smiled and stood to leave, I halted her progress by saying, "Santy?"

"What?"

"If the call for me to sing is great again, what should I do?"

"Tell me. I will help you resist the urge."

"Ta Santy." She attempted a smile, but could not and left all sad-eyed from my room.

I leant back and tried to clear my noggin of thoughts, which was the only thing I excelled at during lessontime. I was glad indeed those days were over. I relished the prospect of attending S.A.N.T. camp for real. Drowsy, I let my lids drop and waited for the numbness of sleep to transport me to another place. Muffled song filtered through my senseless state. I imagined it to be within my skull, so half opened my eyes, expecting the sound to cease. It did not. Fully conscious, I got out of bed and went to the window. I thought myself asleep again and dreaming, for in the distance towards the perimeter fences, I saw lights where no lights should be.

"You see them too?"

Turning, I saw Deogol. He clutched his slabcomp to his chest. With one hand, he pointed at the glass. "They're here. Ghosties heard your song and now they've come to take it back."

"What are you blabbering about?"

He opened up his comp and showed me the screen. Images of white-faced corpses swam around all sorts of textchat. "See? Folk heard a strange noise. I did too. Now all are feared that the dead have risen."

I snatched his slab from him. "Why would they rise?"

"Something bad is going to happen."

"Were you sneaky-peaking just then when I was chatting with Santy?"

"No, I swear."

"On Ma and Da's resting place?"

"Yep. I heard, Adara, I heard. I still hear."

"Hard not to since it is gaining in shrill," I said, took his hand and marched to Santy's room. She was in the hallway and stopped our progress with a furrowed brow.

"See? See what your yearnings have led to Adara?"

"Wha?"

"Praisebees."

"Nah."

"Yes. Praisebees. I heard it too and turned on the visionbox. It would appear that they are at the border fence chanting about the 'Nextgreatsaviour'. Apparently, this being has come to save them from starvation by bringing down the birdies."

"How the huff do they know about that?"

"It's common knowledge that there is a Bringer here. All they had to do was ask a guard if there was an Adara in Cityplace, to confirm their expectations. It does not matter that I have done all I can to promote the falsie that you were named wrong and do not have the skill. Folk within this place believe you are just a girly with too many digits, but outside, your potential is believed."

"Nad and then some."

"I've contacted the mayor. Your identity will be kept secret from tomorrow's lettingloose ceremony. In case some zealot or troublemaker hears it and starts a rumpus. So far as I can tell, you have not been connected to the strange bird-like noise that all folk heard. I gave the mayor a suitable alibi that puts you in the clear."

"But, it wasn't me. I did not…"

"Do not. Do not prolong your lie now that it is out."

I hung my head. Deogol giggled. "Adara, Adara, Adara."

"Not funny," I said and swiped him around the noggin.

"The Praisebees are not a threat, just yet, but if the Agros get wind, then I fear for your safety, I do. Do not look so forlorn. My words are meant to inform not scare. Let us not presume what has not occurred. Go back to bed, pull down the winter blinds, that should block out their ravings. Then go to sleep."

"I'll not be able to, I think."

"Quell your mind jumblings by choosing what you will wear at the ceremony. Now, you, my little Earwig, switch off your comp and get some shut eye." She ruffled Deogol's hair and pushed him towards his restingplace. He sag-shouldered it all the way to his room and slammed the door shut behind him. I shrugged then went to mine.

"Let no one know you sang."

"Not likely Santy." Her warning rattled around my nonce as I headed to my bedchamber.

Once inside I did what she advised and rolled down the heavy-duty wooden slats to muffle the Praisebee chants. It worked a treat and I diverted my gloomy musings by searching my clothesspace for stuff to wear at the ceremony. I fumbled around the rows of pantaloons, skirts, tunics, and all-in-ones.

I didn't have any inner girly sense of what looked appealing when put on, so took out a blue top and black pants. Knowing that the colours would at least not clash with my light blonde hair, and the redder than red face I would assume when all and sundry focused on my bod at the highly visible event.

Putting on said garments, I took a look at my form in the mirror opposite my bed. I was indeed a chunky sight. No manner of tailored or clever material cutting could hide my stocky build. I pulled the belt on my troos and to my surprise found that I needed to yank it tighter to prevent said garment from slipping to the floor. More than one missed meal was taking its toll. Although I flopped my shoulders and let my neck relax with vexation at my unattractive reflection, part of me was glad to be so robust. I stood straight and stared at my image. I was the right proportion for the future I planned.

I was no girlygig for sure. I was a S.A.N.T in the making.

## Chapter Four
*Nothing Ever Happens*

I sat amidst my fellow grads and took to peering around at the assembled throng sitting in the vast auditorium where my lettingloose ceremony was about to begin. It was an echoey place to be sure, well suited for big meetings, or as a venue for travelling thesps and other loudmouths. High of ceiling, made of pale stone, it gave out the vibe of solemn and no mistake.

How could I not sit erect in these stiff-backed chairs that allowed no room for spine slump. Which was what I most earnestly wished to do. My sweat glands were full on with the gravity of the occasion. Plus, my noggin swarmed with Santy's words about the Prasiebees and their desire to make me some kind of hagio. All I wanted to do was to sink into the clean, hard floor and melt away into a puddle of salty stink.

However, I could not. Lettingloose day was a great event that heralded us teens into the ranks of almost 'dult. Meaning, time to choose between a life of procreation, or a kiddless existence in the service of The

Special Army of the New Territories. A Backpacker S.A.N.T. was all I ever wanted to be.

I was keen for this ceremony to be over, as I did not care so much for being plonked amongst so many and was becoming tight of chest. I swear that all of Cityplace was there, except for Deogol, of course. He was worse than me at hating crowds. Never one for the great outdoors, my bro had of late taken to staying inside more often. I could not recall the last time he'd set foot beyond the place we lived in. Except a few moons ago when I saw him skulking near the perimeter fence.

With a greatly sigh, I shuffled in my seat and accidentally touched the arm of Drysi. She glared at me. I turned away, only to face the sneering gob of Hrypa. Just my luck to be seated between the two milksops who had dared me to climb the vidscreen. The same puny pants that had to take back calling me a 'Flimsyfem'.

Drysi whispered into my ear, "I see you couldn't find anything eye-catching to wear. My ma and da procured this fancy outfit for me. It's a Ladies frock, second hand."

"What? You've got a Ladies frock on? An actual dress that a real Lady has worn? I doubt anyone else here has such finery,"

Hrypa shouted out for one and all to hear. He was most aptly named. I do not think the runty juve had the capacity to speak below a bellow. Of course, his yelling attracted the attention of most bods in the place. I managed to slither down in my seat to avoid the backlash of stares that must surely ensue by Hrypa's loud-mouthed exclamation. To my utmost mortification, Drysi stood and turned around so that everyone could witness her most exotic garb. What's more, they all clapped.

"See that Adara, everyone thinks I'm as gorgeous as a Lady." Drysi bowed then sat down. She flicked back her long, curly blonde locks and smoothed out the voluminous skirt that spread around her legs like a thick, pink fog. She turned to me with a smug mush and said in a sweetly voice, "I've got so many Probably's to choose from that I swear I'll have to ask the sheriff to intervene to select the best one for me. I don't know how I'll be able to fend them off and settle down with just one spousemate. I do look forward to becoming a ma and all that."

"Good for you if that's all you want from this brief lifespan."

"Oh Adara, you have turned quite green.

Maybe Hrypa can don a blindfold to become your one and only suitor."

Hrypa pointed at my ever-diminishing form and shouted, "I'd sooner join with a stuffed piggywig thanks."

"You'd get more comfort from said extinct being. There's more yielding to be had in a dead-skin than Adara."

They nearly soiled their undergarments so hard did the limp pair guffaw at my expense. I let them giggle on until they ran out of breath, then said under mine, "You are named right and proper Drysi, for you are indeed a thorny piece of Wolfy puke. As for you, you blabbermouthed excuse for a male, you can have your dead animal and shove it up your..." my words were drowned out by the boom-booming of the Cityplace band that sat in front of the main stage.

I got up from my seat, shoved Hrypa out of his and sat where he once did. Thusly rid of being the filling in their mockery sandwich, I ignored whatever it was he shrieked in my ear, and turned my attention to the crowd. Santy Breanna was there with some oldie relatives. Said ancients were trundled out to such gatherings now and then, otherwise they stayed put in the Goldenagehome.

I waved to Santy, she waved back.

The music stopped.

Sheriff Fychan and Headteach came onto the gold trimmed podium. They bowed and the sheriff, clutching a load of scroll thingy's, stood to one side to let the Headteach do his speechifying. As soon as he opened his gob, my brain went into class mode and switched off. I dare say he gave a goodly talk, but I was lost in thoughts unrelated. All I picked up were a few phrases about the quality and passion of the students, lies, all lies. Then he began to call us up. Nad.

One by one the grinning juves walked onto the stage, shook his hand, grabbed the paper tube from the sheriff, then walked back down the few steps to their original places. I waited for my turn, wondering what tag he would use to summon me. "A. Baird."

Ouch and then some. I shot out of my seat and legged it up the stairs in no more than two jumps. I grabbed Headteach's hand and gave it a vigorous shake. Sheriff Fychan plonked a rolled up piece of paper in my mitt. I quickly left, but not back to my allotted seat. I'd spied Santy and my other oldie relative sitting to the side of the musicians. Quick as a sneeze, I made my way to them, unravelling the scroll as I went. It was blank. What the huff was that all about?

I gave a quickly nod to my greatgranma. "Adala, don't you look as cute as a kittle with a ribbon on?"

"It's Adara, Greatgrangran," I said in a whisper, bending low so only she could hear.

"That's what I said."

"No, you said…" Santy poked me in the ribs and I stood. She squinted and pouted like a girlybub. I smiled at my grey haired greatgranma. In a louder voice, said, "How are you?" Blunder of the highest order. Santy rolled her eyes and I clenched my teeth.

"Oh, I'm the same. Nothing ever changes. Nothing happens. Everyday is the same. I get up, I eat, I watch a few vids, then play some game I don't know how to play, then I eat again and sleep. It's a boring life. But that's to be expected. I've served my purpose. Now I'll just have to wait for the last great moment, and fumble off this mortal soil."

"Coil."

"What?"

Another poke by Santy. "Nowt."

Grangran made her mouth even thinner than it was. "Have you made a joining yet?"

"No Greatgrangran."

"Adela, you've got to get going on that. Why I was younger than you by an orbit or more when I chose your greatgranda. He always said that he spotted me first, but I'd been eyeballing him for many orbits."

Although I kept my face relaxed and assumed a countenance of interest, my insides screamed to flee. Granny Amranwen spurted out the exact same blabberings every time I saw her. Which was no more than twice an orbit at most; thank the sky and all the stars in it. Still, I knew she would babble on until a tasty was brought before her.

I nudged Santy. She fumbled in her side pocket for something to distract her. To my relief, Santy held forth a luscious bar of Sterichoc. Granny Amranwen snatched it from her hand, tore off the red crinkly wrapper and stuffed half the thing into her drooling mouth. I turned away when the brown sweetie stuff began to melt and ooze down her chin. Quicker than a bumble collecting pollen, two staffnursies from Goldenagehome, rose from their seats, produced a Steriwipe each, in one swift movement, they'd cleaned her face.

"Mind what you are doing Meilyr, I nearly choked. Where are the puppets?"

"No puppets today, Ma. It's the lastday ceremony of the ripe ones. Remember?' Meilyr said. The big staffnursey bent down to where she was sitting and took her frail hand in his. How fragile her small fingers looked in his great paws. Aptly named 'ironman' this 'dult. For I have seen him lift two male juves right up into the air, one in each hand, when they said a rude thing about one of his oldies.

"Ah, waste of time. I wanted to see the puppets. If I'd known it was only Aledra's lastday thingy, I'd have stayed put, played 'gokittlego' on my new slab gizmo." We all laughed. She tutted. "Like I said, it's a boring life. Nothing ever happens."

I became aware of a rumbling sound, not unlike thunder. I turned to Santy Breanna and saw her tear off down the central aisle towards the main door. Greatgrangran folded her arms and let her head drop onto her chest. I strained my neck to see what was going on.

"Our time is nigh. Prepare to meet your maker. Make peace with the BabyCheesus and repent your slovenly ways!"

Huffin' hell, Praisebees.

Santy Breanna was pushed backwards by two burly guards as a whole load of Christfans burst into the building. They wore long flowing tunics tied loosely around the waist by some raggedy rope. They flipped-flopped their way towards the stage with scanty sandals that exposed chipped and mucky toenails. They showed their teeth. I'd never seen such dirty dental prongs before. All were tarnished brown, with stuff that looked like flesh, stuck between them. Some gouged out the sinuous bits with their jagged fingernails and popped the remnant into their mouths to be swallowed with relish. So, not just Praisebees then? Were these fanatics Carnies too? I shuddered.

A loud gasp and a general putting of hands over mouths ensued when the bedraggled worshippers walked past. Santy attempted to force her way through the Praisebee guards, but they were huge and stood in front of her like the trunks of trees.

The sheriff and Headteach, who were still on the stage, huddled together and looked around for some kind of security backup. Sheriff Fychan, a small thin male without much hair, yanked out a comdevice and screamed down it for assistance. He threw the thing onto the floor when all it did was make a buzzing noise. He peeled the Headteach's arms from around his waist. Stepping forward, he said, "Stop right where you are. Advance no further. I said, stop!"

But the Praisebees did not. They tramped faster chanting, "Cheesus is life. Cheesus is good. Believe in him and live forever."

A catchy little ditty to be sure, but it fell upon deaf ears. All in Cityplace believed in the OneGreatProvider that centuries ago saved the few remaining bigwigs from famine and disease. He built our now great home where we live, safe and sound. Except that today, we were not. The leader of the group walked up the steps and onto the stage. Sheriff Fychan held up his hands in front of his chest to warn the tall slim male, to advance no further. The 'dult smacked his mitts away. He turned to the quaking crowd.

"Calm yourselves. Do not be so a-feared. We come in peace. We come because of rumours."

Nad.

"Word has filtered through to our nomadic ears that the dead and lost ones have risen."

Double nad.

"That these troubled spirits have come to warn us of things to come. Things most wretched and horrible. We must listen to them. Mend our ways. If not, then all upon this land-starved planet will perish once and for all. If that is so, then a saviour must rise to save folk. That hagio, or saint, will free us from despair and deprivation. That saviour is here."

Triple nad.

The Praisebee/Carnie disciples fell to their knees and banged their heads upon the hard, stone floor, saying as one, "Praisebee Cheesus. Praisebee Cheesus." Blood from their temple wounds splattered just about everywhere. Cityfolk gasped with terror and disgust at their pristine, clean space being tainted by their red disease-ridden fluids. Santy used this distraction to rush past the guards and join me.

Hrypa started the screaming and near all joined in. Except for myself, Santy Breanna and Greatgrangran, who was still asleep. Santy grabbed my wrist and pulled me through the standing audience. She nodded to Meilyr, who shook Greatgran Amranwen until she woke. He helped her rise and pushed her through the shrieking folk that stood before their chairs. The main Praisebee lifted his arms to the ceiling. Something heavy fell through the skylight in the roof.

The head-pounding Cheesus/Carnie nuts, put their hands under their robes and drew out facemasks. They pressed them over their noses and mouth, then joined their leader on the stage. I was baffled by their action until I saw the grey vapour spread around the room. The screaming stopped. Coughing started.

Gas bombs.

## Chapter Five
*The Truth About Ghosties*

My eyes streamed with stinging water and my lungs near burst for lack of fresh air. When I did suck in a lungful, I hacked and wheezed. After more than a few secs, the smoke dispersed. I saw a sea of hands and legs as folk attempted to crawl to the nearest exit.

Above the choking sounds, the voice of the main Praisebee could be heard going on about that Baby huffin' Cheesus, how he died for our sins and such stuff. I would have shouted back something along the lines of, "Yeah he sounds like a great 'dult all right, but how long ago was he alive? Oh, and what about the old-old saying, 'Practice what you preach.'" I think your Cheesus would be very upset with your behaviour here, don't you?" But all I did was spit up gunge.

"And the Lord said unto his children, 'Let those without sin cast the first stone.' His mighty words humbled those around him and made them think twice before accusing others of things they may well have done themselves. That is what we must do, since we are all His children. Soon to become hungry. Hungry for the taste of that which has been denied us for too long. We need more than grain for sustenance. We need flesh."

His ranting became even less coherent as he continued to blast out his version of all things Christian and the desire for meat. The other devotees wailed and slapped their thighs. Then looked to the ceiling with a look of ecstatic joy upon their pale faces. I sat back on my heels, wiped my face on the sleeve of my tunic before twitching violently as a Steriwipe was pressed against my neck. I turned. Greatgrangran was on her knees holding said cloth. Her face was screwed up and tears streaked down her wrinkled face. She coughed a few times then said, "Here, use the thing to cool down the inflammation around your eyes Andrea."

"Ta," I said, took the wipe from her and held it against my closed lids. It did indeed reduce the itchiness. I was able to stand and help Greatgrangran to her feet. "Where is Meilyr?"

"How should I know? We got separated when everyone fell to the floor all gasping for breath. Good job I came out with my oxymask. I was going to leave it behind, I haven't needed it for ages now, but you know what? Something in my bones told me to take it with me."

"Goodly good for you Grangran."

She squinted in the direction of the stage, where the Praisebees still stood, and tutted loudly. "Foolish zealots. What do they want do you think?"

I had an inkling from what they said before letting off the gas bomb, but I did not want to disturb Greatgrangran, so I threw her a whopper instead. "Don't know. Maybe they just want to convert us to the ways of the BabyCheesus."

"All blarney. I don't believe in all that holierthanthou stuff. I believe in what I see before me, not in mythical if's and what's. I'd sooner pray to the Greenman than a long dead bub from who knows where. Besides, they are not real believers. I've not heard of the Praisebees courting violence and advocating the consumption of meat. Plah! They are nothing more than Carnies out to hoodwink."

Despite the nasty predicament we were in, I could not help but snicker at Grangran's take on things. She may have been an oldie but she was, for sure, no mushbrainer. The Carnies were about and no mistake. They'd just latched onto a few extremists to gain access into Cityplace. Yep, they were shifty and then some.

I searched the room for Santy Breanna. But there were too many bods all staggering about for me to see anything clearly. I would have called her name, but there would be no point. What with all the moaning, crying, and the chief Praisebee banging on about this and that, I doubt my voice would have been heard.

The noisiness ended 'bruptly when the curfew chime sounded. Everyone became still, quiet as a stuffed moocow on display. I looked towards the stage area. One of the Praisbee guards shoved a pointy stick into the sheriff's back, by way of forcing him to ring said alarm again. When he shook his head, the guard twisted one of his arms so high up his back that I thought it would snap in two. Sheriff Fychan rang the bell. The main Praisebee raised his hands in the air. The others that remained banging their heads, stood and joined him on the stage, blood dripping from their open wounds.

"Good folk of Cityplace, please, please be seated."

Like kiddles in class, we did.

He walked to the front of the platform.

"Good citizens, allow me first to apologise for the necessity to use a mild force in order to attain your full attention. The bombs and the substances they contained are harmless irritants only, they will have no lasting damage."

He stopped and gestured to a male and fem that were not head damaged. They stepped out from the line of red splattered Praisbees, and stood either side of him. "My name is Daniel. Together with my friends Elijah and Lilith, we come to share our faith. To talk about the dead rising. The last great sign of the end of all things. That and the outing of the Auger."

A general murmuring swept around the room. I hunched myself up as best I could in the stiff chair.

"Now, I am sure that you will have many questions. When you have heard me out, I will be glad indeed to answer them as best I can."

Greatgrangran tugged my arm. I leant in close to her. She whispered, "Look to the far left of the room."

I did and saw Santy Breanna with one of the boarder guards. She was gesticulating to someone at the opposite end of the chamber. I turned my head in the direction she pointed, and there by the back exit, two S.A.N.T.S. stood in full battle dress. I hid my grin behind my hand. These Praisebee/Carnies had better be quick with their explanations before the S.A.N.T.S. let rip and brought them to their knees. I put my arm around Greatgrangran. She chuckled like a bub with a chocopop.

"Dear beloved, folk of Cityplace, we are here to tell you the news. To help you to let God into your bosoms and go to the great heavenplace above with a pure heart and soul. Become one of us. God will open up the pearlygates and you shall reside forever in the kingdom of heaven. Praise the Lord!" His voice swelled on the last sentence. All the other followers repeated it several times. "The dead have risen. Soon there will be a storm. A raging wind and violent shuddering that will destroy us all. Let us give you the chance to save your souls, to find the Adara, who will bring the birdybirds to us. Then we shall feast on forgotten flesh. So it was told, so shall it be, so shall…"

Thankfully, Daniel did not finish his somewhat repetitive speech. A rope was flung around his, Elijah's, and Lilith's chest, pinning their arms to their sides. The next instant, they were flat on the floor, The

S.A.N.T.S. I had seen but a moment before, were standing over them.

Santy Breanna leapt onto the stage, grabbed the guard that had made Sheriff Fychan press the curfew chime, and held a knife to his throat. Before the other Prasiebee muscle could intervene, the fem S.A.N.T. kicked the back of his knees bringing him down with a thud. She pressed her foot upon his neck so that he could not move. An enormous cheer spread around the place. As one bod, we all stood and shrieked until our throats became hoarse.

The other followers backed away, but were prevented from fleeing the scene by the male S.A.N.T. who let rip a restraining cord that swished around their bods and held them fast in a huddled glob. Daniel writhed in his bondage and spat out some sort of profanity about worshiping false idols. Santy Breanna cuffed the Praisebee guard then pushed him down next to the prostrate Cheesus disciples.

She stood tall and addressed the arena, "All is clear, I think. Clear, and safe again. Dreng and Orva are to thank for scuppering these zealots misguided intentions. It is goodly indeed to know that these brave soldiers of the Special Army of the New

Territories, are within a bub's breath of our home and in a sec, can be here when trouble begins."

Another cheer caused said S.A.N.T.S. to wave to the crowd. They lifted Daniel, Lilith, and Elijah, and pushed them to the front of the stage. Santy walked up to them and pulled Daniel to face the auditorium.

We sat down all calm as if we were about to see an entertainment. Santy spoke, "I believe these so-called Praisebees, are not what they seem. All this chat of meat and the like, has given them away. They are Carnies, not believers in the BabyCheesus. What we do with these folk and how they shall be punished, is up to the sheriff and law enforcers of our city. But I dare say a night spent in the filth hole and a trip to the Decontamination place will be a start."

Yet another cheer. Santy Breanna was a goodly speaker indeed. "However, they came here because of rumours." No cheer this time, just a shuffling of feet. "These rumours spread fast and far. Such goss must cease. If these misguided ones heard so much whilst only moving on foot, then you can be sure those with eyes and ears in every part of this sad land, will have heard also. Agros could use this info against us. They could fuel our fears and make us do who knows what."

Sheriff Fychan, supporting his left arm with his right hand, approached Santy. "Fine and noble words Breanna, but fact is fact. These 'rumours' may not be mere fabrication. I heard the sound, as did we all. The Praisbees, or Carnies in disguise, are misguided but they are right. We do have an Adara, I know you put it about that she was wrongly named, but was she? What about the eerie noises last moonrise? The dead are rising, talking. That can mean only one thing."

His last words were drowned out by several girlygig shrieks, quickly joined and made more piercing, by most of the crowd shouting and yelling. I put my hand over my ears. Greatgrangran stuffed her fingers down her hearing holes. Santy Breanna waved her hands to indicate all should cease their bellyaching, and after a sec or two, all did. Someone shouted out, "This is terrible. We are doomed. We must contact the Agros and ask for their help."

"When have the Agros ever helped us?" Santy said.

There was a general muttering of, "Well, never," then all went quiet again.

The sheriff spoke, "The Agros are the least of our worries. The Lost Ones are restless, they have come to claim their interest. Kiddles are going missing. Meeks are took."

"That is myth."

"Is it Breanna?"

"Yes. It is. Oh, I know the teachings of the OneGreatProvider and the stuff about one day folk paying for the comfort and joy he gave us."

"By the taking of as many now that were saved then. Famine will reign where once was bounty. An Auger will rise and end the hunger. But not before many have died."

A massive gasp ripped through the place and even the bound Praisebees gave over to wide-eye.

Voices called out for sacrifices to soothe the founder of Cityplace. Greatgrangran got quite animated when a young 'un said, "Let him have the oldies."

I felt as heavy as if I'd eaten our entire stock of oatleys in one sitting, and mumbled so no one could hear, "It wasn't the dead it was me calling to the birdybirds."

"What? What did you say, Adara?"

Finally, Grangran got my name right, I thought. Then I thought, oops.

"Now then, have you been practising your namegift?"

"Well, maybe."

Greatgran Amranwen stood, and impressively for one of her age, stepped up onto her chair. She waved her arms around. Santy Breanna called for hush and all turned to Grangran. I tried to say something but she 'shushed' me to silence. "You fools. You'll believe in all sorts of silliness that's for sure. Dead rising, my saggy butt. There were never any ghosties about. It was Ad…"

"Amranwen, Granmam, quiet!" Santy yelled and raced down the stairs towards her.

"Don't tell me to shush girly. As I was saying, no ghosties in Cityplace, just Adara, singing to the birdies."

HUFFIN' HELL!

## Chapter Six
*Saved By The Seat Of My Pantaloons.*

Santy stopped at the bottom of the stage area. Greatgrangran smiled, held her hand out for me to take so that I could help her down. She huffed and puffed with the effort then sat back on her seat as though nowt had happened. Sheriff Fychan looked at Santy then at me. "What have you to do with all this young 'un?"

I shrugged, made a twirling motion with my forefinger next to my head and pointed at Grangran. Unfortunately for me, she noticed.

"You impudent little aphid. Trying to suggest that I'm not all there in the brain section."

She stood and I hoped that she would not try to climb onto her seat again. I was deep in face red as it was. "I'll tell you what she has to do with all of this. You stay where you are Breanna. Glad you are defending Adler, but the truth must out if these halfwits are to cease their grip on these ghost and ghoulie tales. Stand up girly." I did not so she gave me a sharp poke in the ribs with her bony fingers.

"Ow, that hurts."

"Good, now stand."

I did. I swear my skin was the colour of the setting sun. I stared at the stage and saw Sheriff Fychan's face turn a dark shade of purple. "Tell all you know olddame."

"Olddame? Humph! I have a name young 'un, just like you do. I suggest you use it when addressing someone of my advancing years and experience."

"Apologies Amranwen, please continue."

"Little Adwela."

"Adara."

"Of course it is. Little Adara is the cause of said nighttime noises that have given all such a scare. She has been singing to the birdybirds as her namegift impels her to do."

Santy put her hand over her face and I felt my shoulders droop. Daniel and the other pretend Praisebees began to snicker. Sheriff Fychan tugged on their bonds until they stopped. A mumbling, grumbling rolled throughout the gathered and I picked out one or two phrases that I'd rather have not heard.

"Catcher of Birds."

"Meat Bringer. She can serve us."

"My 'nuncle's a Carnie, hiding out near the Woodsfolk camp. In with the Agros he is. When I give him this info I can barter with him and get that 3D replicator I saw in a tech mag."

"Get her to bring down all the birybirds. Then we can have a real feast. Why should the Carnies have all the fun?"

"We can sell her to the Agros. Then we'll never go without."

So it continued. My head buzzed with talk of how folk could use me for their ill-gotten gains. The hubbub grew. The hundreds of Citydwellers that had sat so placid throughout this ordeal, rose as one and moved in on Greatgrangran and myself.

Before I could grab her and rush to safety, the mass of greedy folk had surrounded us. I began to wonder whether the Carnie's gas bomb was fuelled with some kind of mind-bending drug to make these sissy's crave flesh so. I called to Santy and thought I heard her call back, but I couldn't be sure such was the din coming from the throats of my potential attackers.

"What's going on? Get your silly selves away from me and mine," Grangran said and started swatting folk with her niknakbag.

I took a defensive stance. Jabbed out at those that tried to grab me. Santy trained me well. I was goodly indeed when up against a scrap. Only two full moons ago I defeated all and sundry at the illegal 'Rough House Games.' However, then unlike now, my assailants attacked individually, not on mass. I felt many hands grip onto my arms, legs and shoulders. Before I could protest at the outrage of it all, I was lifted up into the air and carried towards the exit.

I wriggled and they flipped me over so that I saw the floor instead of the ceiling. I was jiggled about so much that my innards spun and tumbled, for a sec I thought that I would barf. Then I heard a familiar voice say, "You there, put her down, now. If you do not, I swear by the OneGreatProvider, I and the other S.A.N.T.S. will rope you like the Praisebees."

"You can try if you like," someone said. I heard a dull thud, then I was dropped.

However, I did not fall flat on my face, as two outstretched arms caught me before I hit the ground. Meilyr held me close. I wrapped my arms around him and almost shed a tear. "Quickly, get her out of the building," Santy said. I lifted my head and saw her thwack and wallop folk after folk that tried to yank me from the staffnursy's grip. Yep, that gas contained something nasty all right. These placid dwellers were out for blood.

Meilyr let me down, holding onto me with

one arm whilst striking out with the other each time a hand reached towards my bod. I kicked, spat and clawed at anyone who came near. But they were as if possessed by the very phantoms they believed had risen. Despite mine, Santy's, and Meilyr's best efforts, I was ripped and dragged away from his protective grip and hauled backwards by the belt with astonishing speed. I thought I would take off.

The Cityfolk swarmed after.

Orva appeared from who knows where, gave me a thumbs up sign, then turned and fired a barrage of small pellets at the advancing mob. They fell to the ground, hands over their head, yelling as if they had been smacked with a tree trunk. We came to a halt. A strong arm swivelled me around, hauled me up and onto their shoulders. I looked down at the upturned face smiling at me. "Ta." Dreng gave me a wink and ran full pelt up the steps.

Orva followed close behind, pushing the Headteach and the sheriff to the ground. Then she pressed a button that I thought would activate the curfew bell, but to my surprise, saw a door open at the back of the stage. Dreng put me down and whispered in my ear, "Run as fast as you can. We will be right behind ye. Don't stop until ye reach the end wall." He pushed me. I did as he said and ran into the dark space.

It was too dim for me to get a clear look at where I was. I stretched my arms out to the side and touched wall. It was a corridor that led to somewhere. I wondered briefly, why it was there, and if the sheriff knew about it. All thoughts on the matter ceased when I heard raised voices behind me. More than two. I ran faster, hands before my face so that I didn't come a cropper on something ahead, then came to an abrupt halt when they hit something hard.

"Adara? Are ye well?"

"Yep."

"Stay where ye are."

"Not likely to do otherwise."

"Of course. I am lighting a gas tube, so do not be alarmed at the strange noise ye are about to hear."

A crackling, hissing sound filled the space and the dimness diminished. Through the hazy glow, I saw Dreng, Orva and two more shadowy figures. I blinked and rubbed my eyes. There before them were not only the S.A.N.T.S. but two of the Carnie/Praisebees.

"What the huffin' heck are they doing here?"

"They must have followed us through. Although I do not know how they managed to free themselves."

"Why, we prayed to Cheesus. He came to our aid."

"No, he did not. Lilith carries a small blade with her at all times. She managed to wriggle it free, I stooped down, picked it up and she cut her bonds then mine. We were not noticed because of the disruption taking place."

Lilith gave Elijah a somewhat less than Christian look and sucked in her cheeks. Elijah bowed. Orva cuffed him about the noggin. "You should not be here. You are trouble. I cannot send you back, as much as I wish to. We cannot let you be found and blab about this not-so-secret passage. You will have to come with us."

"Which is where?"

"Ah, now that would be telling, Adara. It is enough ye know that we are taking ye to a safe place until all this hoo-ha blows over."

"Will it?"

"Who knows? Not even the Greenman himself would attempt to second guess the strange ways of folk in Cityplace."

Dreng's accent was oddly indeed. Clearly he was not from here.

"Dreng, you are not a born-and-bred Citydweller?"

"Oh, very well spotted Adara. Nay I am a Woodsfolk male firstly. S.A.N.T. second and last."

Wow! He was a Woodsmale. They have a reputation for being tough and smelly. I sniffed and took in my own fear stink. He did not exude anything nasty. Perhaps that came from the S.A.N.T. training.

"Enough chat. Dreng, activate the unlocking device."

He pulled out a small round black box and pressed it with his thumb. A whirring noise gave over to a clanking sound. The dead-end before us became a long narrow tunnel that dipped sharply downwards. "I'll gae first to light the way. Orva wi bring the rear. Adara, wi follow me. The rest gae in single file behind her. This is a steep incline, slippery in parts. Be wary. Tread careful. If ye fall, we wi not be able to save ye, so acute is the drop."

Dreng thrust the gas tube light before him then entered the passage. He stopped at the top of a rickety looking wooden staircase and motioned for me to follow. I turned to the others and repeated the gesture he made to me. For a moment, I felt as if I too were a

S.A.N.T. and became less a-feared fuelled by my brief brush with responsibility. It lasted less than a sec, for when I stepped towards Dreng, my foot caught on something. I tripped and fell into his arms. He guffawed most deeply and helped me right myself. I was thankful the place was so dark for I felt a heat burst most prominently across my face and neck.

The Woodsmale S.A.N.T. grabbed onto the rail that jutted out from the wall and made his way down the creaky steps. I followed close not daring to see how the others fared, in case I lost my footing once again. The light from Dreng's torch was adequate enough, but I discovered that if I did not keep up with his robust pace, I was plunged into almost darkness. Thankfully Orva's torch at the rear cast a dim glow that was sufficient to illuminate the narrow tunnel.

We wended our way in silence. The air became humid. I found it difficult to take in enough lungfuls and had to stop once or twice to catch my breath. On one occasion, Elijah caught up with me. He spoke low into my ear, "You are well? Not suffering from fright at all things dark, deep and confined?"

"Nope, just find it a tad difficult to fill my

air sacs. Do you have a phobe about such things?"

He shook his head vigorously and gulped. I could tell by the droplets of fear-wet on his brow that he was not telling the truth. I admired his pluckiness in the face of such a trial as this, and patted him on the shoulder. "Stay up close with me. If you slip or falter, then I will be a buffer. You shall not fall."

If he had been taller or stouter than myself, I would not have offered to use my bod to protect him, but seeing as he was as lean as a twig and most bereft of muscle power, I felt secure in making him the offer.

"I accept your most generous proposal in the good spirit it is given and will endeavour to not use it."

This Carnie/Praisebee was different from the rest. He did not exude the meat raving antsy of the other cravers. I wondered if he were all Praisebee and not much Carnie after all. All curious in the extreme, I sucked in as much air as was available, and continued the precarious descent to who knows where.

## Chapter Seven
*Beneath Cityplace*

I could hear Elijah's rapid breathing become strained the deeper we plunged below the city, and hoped that we were close to our destination. I feared that he might collapse before we reached it, so turned my head to see if he was well. He gulped many times, holding tightly onto the rail. On seeing my concerned expression, he attempted a tiny smile. I raised my eyebrows, showed him my teeth, and looked over his shoulder to the shadowy figures of Orva and Lilith.

Said Praisebee had long dark hair that fell to her waist. Although it looked somewhat unwashed, it was thick and straight. In the half-light, she resembled an image I had seen in worshipclass of what the Christians called, 'The Virgin.'

Orva raised her torch. "There, look Adara, we are almost at the bottom."

I took a few steps down and peered into the gloominess. Dreng stopped, waved his light at the space before him and lit up a vast cavern with many arched grottos that I assumed led to more tunnels. I quickened my pace and was soon by his side, closely followed by a panting Elijah, Lilith, and Orva. "We are below Cityplace, utterly out of sight. These are secret tunnels that only a few know about."

"How come you do?"

"Ah, well, you see, all S.A.N.T.S. know about these, Adara."

"What even Santy Breanna?"

"It wa she who sent us down here."

"You intimated others are aware of this wondrous place," Elijah said.

"I am not at liberty to divulge such info. Ye must know that we cannae allow ye to blab of this to anyone once we have left."

Elijah looked at Lilith who shook her head. "In all faith, we cannot promise such a thing. This is such an important find. One that will give us great standing with our own."

"Who are? Praisebees or Carnies?" I said folding my arms all-haughty like.

Elijah scratched his matted hair, blew air though his teeth, then looked to Lilith. She squinted and said, "We are Praisebees, first and foremost. True, some have taken to Carnie ways, but none have veered from the path of righteousness."

"Really? Would it be right then to blab about this place? If so, for what purpose?"

"So many questions, Adara, too many to answer now. Know that we detest secrecy and this place, kept only for a select few, is wrong by our faith values. It should be open for all in times of Agro aggression."

In truth, I could not find anything wrong in what Lilith said. This cavern and its potential as a hideout from threat should indeed be accessible for all.

Orva bowed her head for a sec, then gave us a serious look. "Do not question further. Dreng and I have nothing against you, or your people so long as you abide with the laws we live by. Today you and yours broke these rulings. Those left behind will be brought to justice. We must also arrange a suitable punishment for you both. If you promise to keep shtum, we will forego the retribution. You shall not be harmed. What do you say?"

Lilith jutted out her chin and her fellow Praisebee looked to the floor. "I can only talk for myself. I do not find the notion of punishment a thing to fear. I am prepared to die for my belief. Do what you must. I will not keep info from my brothers and sisters."

All attention turned to Elijah. He coughed. "I do not know how giving the whereabouts of this place to one and all would be of benefit to our cause. It is an empty cave, what would we do with it?"

"It is secret and must not be. All folk would wish to know that it is here. It could be of use."

"I do not see its relevance to our cause. In fact, it may generate unrest amongst us. We do not want more."

Lilith opened her mouth, then closed it again. Elijah put his hand on her shoulder and stared into her dark brown eyes. "We will not tell. No reason to. Indeed, as a thank you for allowing us to flee the situation above, I feel it is only right to pay you back for your generosity. Is that not so Lilith?" She nodded.

"I fear you do not possess anything we need. All Good?" We nodded. "Then let us continue."

Dreng held up his hand. "Wait but a sec Orva. It is most gratifying to hear ye say these words Elijah, but I think it may be best if both ye and Lilith are blindfolded for the rest of the way."

"Soundly plan. Do not protest. Do not fear for your safety. I will take hold of Lilith, Dreng shall take Elijah. You will come to no harm."

The Praisebees offered no struggle when

Orva pulled out two long pieces of black cloth, handed one to Dreng and placed one across Lilith's eyes. He did the same to Elijah and in synchronisation they tied the blindfolds tight. "Now we can continue."

This time Orva, led the way, illuminating the darkness with a bright light from her torch. She held onto Lilith's hand and marched onwards with a quickly pace. Lilith tottered for a moment, but managed to keep up with Orva's long stride. Dreng motioned me to follow and pulled Elijah with him. On we walked across the vast cavern. It was like nothing I had seen before. In the flickering light, I saw how roughly the place had been hewn. The stone looked as if it had been hacked by blunt objects. I slowed my pace till Dreng came up beside me. "Why do ye loiter so?"

"I am in awe is all. Do you know who constructed this place?"

"Nay. All we know is what we are told in camp. That it was most likely formed at the same time as Cityplace. Perhaps as an escape route if there was any Agro trouble. To my knowledge, few have used it. There having never been a need tae."

"Until now."

"Indeed. Come on lassie, nay time for

viewing."

Dreng nudged my elbow and we continued onwards until we came to one of the holes at the far end of the cave. All stopped. "These tunnels are narrow and low. You must bend a little to pass through," Orva said. She let go of Lilith, motioned for me to follow her a little away from the rest, so I did. She put her finger to her lips and said all whispery, "You are to hide out here until things quieten above."

"How long will that take? It's not as if me and my name can just disappear all sudden like and not be noticed."

"Folk are easily diverted. The Praisebee trial will occupy their thoughts. Then all will be well. Down that passage is a room especially built for such an occasion. It has supplies. In fact, everything you will need to keep you safe until we come for you. But, you must share it with the Praisebees. It was not our plan for them to be here. I am sorry."

"Can't say that I relish the idea of being confined below ground with two zealots. What if they try to escape?"

Orva ran her fingers through her short blonde hair. She reached down her trouser leg, opened a side pocket and withdrew a nifty looking blade. "This is an all-purpose knife. It is sharp on one side, serrated on the other. I know that your have been trained by Breanna to use such a weapon. I feel confident that if the need arises you will do so with great efficiency and not hesitate."

I took the thing from her and hid it the inner pocket of my tunic. "If needs be I will."

"Good. Either Dreng or myself will come with news and provisions." Orva smiled, headed back to Lilith and took her hand. "Come, we are almost at our destination." She led us through a long winding tunnel that led onto a narrow corridor, and pointed at a hollow at the end of it. "That is our destination."

"We have trodden quite a ways. Have you taken us to a different location?"

Orva raised her eyebrows and winked. "Could be Lilith. Who knows where you are?" Impressivo. She was fast at taking advantage of situations. A goodly idea to confuse the Praisebees, in case they did have the opportunity to blab about this place.

We strode to the gap. Orva spoke, keeping up the falsehood, "We are within another building. This is where you shall remain until it is safe for you to leave. Please do not try to escape. Adara has been given full authority to use whatever force is necessary to prevent this happening. Besides, there is nowhere for you to go."

"Have you taken us to the Wilderness? Or even, the Beyondness?"

"The Beyondness? That place is too far away, fool," Lilith said.

"Sorry, but we are not at liberty to divulge such info."

"Nay more talk. Move," Dreng said and we walked into the small corridor.

As we entered, the place was lit up by a series of tiny lights above our heads. Both S.A.N.T.S. extinguished their torches and placed them into their backpouches. It was unlike the other corridor in every way. The walls were smooth and painted white. The ceiling was high and not at all rough. Air circulated around it as if we were in Centralplaza itself. It was a cooling breeze and if I too had my eyes covered, I would have believed myself in a well-ventilated building rather than an underground cavern.

Dreng waved to me. I went to him. He put Elijah's hand in mine. "I must lock the outer door. You are in charge of this male and that fem, Adara," he said, walked back to the hole we came in, pressed something above the entrance and it sealed shut.

"What is happening?"

"Nowt Elijah, keep walking."

He did. Soon we caught up with Orva and Lilith. They were standing before a wooden door at the far end of the passage. She waited for Dreng then spoke, "You may remove your blindfolds." They did and blinked a few times. "That is where you will be residing. It is a large room with many comforts. Adara is in charge. She will have access to a comdevice."

"I will?"

"Yes," she said and took one from her sleeve pouch. "Only use it when absolutely necessary. We have no info on who may be able to access its frequency. It is a last resort only."

"I understand. Ta."

Orva went to the door and pulled it open. A bright light came on and I thought for a sec that I was back in Cityplace. Before us was a large room set out exactly like the living area at home. We went in and I was relieved to observe that there were four sleeping areas. The only difference was that instead of the usual foodprep room, there was another wooden door. Dreng stood by it.

"This is where we will leave and enter. It will be locked at all times. Only Orva and myself have the means to open it."

I looked at the Praisebees. They had a blank expression as if what was occurring where a dream. "Where are we to cook and eat?"

"No cooking, Adara. There is foodstuff enough in that box on the shelf by the sofa. Inside are water, soylygrub, Sterichoc…"

"Sterichoc! Mine, all of it," I said and dove into the contents of said box. I was somewhat dismayed that there was only one bar, but did not hesitate to eat it right then and there. I wiped my mouth. "Sorry, but I have not tasted this sweety stuff in many moons."

Orva grinned. "The provisions were meant to be replenished, but with all of the hoo-ha, there was no one spare to attend to this necessity. You will have to share what there is until we can bring more. This may not be as quickly as you would wish, so please be cautious in your portions."

I felt a pang of guilt, then caught sight of a small sachet of Yellowsweet and held it out to Elijah and Lilith. "Sorry for the fastly consumption of our only choc. Here, you can have the vanilla curd."

Lilith smiled and took the sachet from me. She opened it, squeezed some into her mouth then handed it to Elijah. He greedily drank it dry and sighed. "We have not fed for a sunup or two."

This I well believed, for in the brightness of the room I clearly saw their sunken eyes, hollow cheeks and thinner than thin arms. Some, however, had eaten of fleshly bits, as I observed in the auditorium before. These two? Nah, far too narrow of wrist to be Carnies.

"We must leave. We will return as soon as. Hopefully, with good news. Until then, be calm," Orva said. She and Dreng went to the doorway. They nodded to us, pushed the door open then stepped through.

"Dae not despair," Dreng said and pulled the door shut behind him.

## Chapter Eight
*Not All The Comforts Of Home*

Lilith flopped onto the comfycouch. As her head fell back, she closed her eyes and let out a low groan. Elijah sank onto the matching cream coloured recliner, and placed his hands on the arms of the chair. I remained standing not knowing exactly what to say.

A few secs elapsed with us all in the same position, before I spoke, "So, I suppose we should choose a slumberroom each. What with all the excitement and the like, I need to cleanse. But then, I will have to dress in what I am now wearing, which may well be infused with my perspiration. I could rinse said garment, but then would need to hide my almost nakedness until it dried. That I could do in the privacy of my chamber, so, all in all, that is what I propose to do."

My inane babblings fell upon ears that were not attuned to my voice. I stared at their bland faces expressing nowt but fatigue, Elijah gave out a loud yawn.

"It has been many days and nights since I slept. Daniel kept us awake chanting and praying so that we would be ready for the assault on Cityplace."

Lilith snapped her eyes open. She raised her head and said, "Elijah, sshh, say nothing more. He is confused through lack of sleep for sure. Of course, we only heard about the ghostie thing but yesterday, so could not have been preparing prior to that."

I folded my arms and gave them an all-knowing stare. Elijah stood, too quickly as it turned out, for he lost his balance and fell to his knees. He made a high-pitched wheezing noise then put his head in his hands and blubbed loudly. Lilith sighed. "He is weak. Daniel knew that. That is why he decided to choose him as a group leader. To give him authority in the hope it would toughen him up so that this kind of display would not occur." She shook her head, crossed her legs and gave out another sigh of contempt.

"Tell me more of this planned incursion."

"There is no more to be said."

I knelt next to Elijah and put my hand on his shaking shoulder. He lifted his tear-streaked face, gulped a few times then ceased to blub. I dug into my pants pocket and handed him a Wipeclean. He dabbed it around his face for a bit before offering the soiled cloth back.

"Erm, no ta, just fling into the wastebin in the…" I glanced at the space where such a device would have been, but saw nowt but white wall. "Keep it in your mitts until I locate a place for disposing of all things impure."

I stood and searched the room, but found no holes to rid ourselves of any muck we might gather during our stay. Flummoxed, I went into the slumberrooms . I almost cried out. They were just that. Rooms fit only for sleep. Each space contained a bed, small table and chair. Nowt else. No steamshower much to my great vexation. I began to panic somewhat and went into the tiny box-like hallway that separated all the rooms.

To my greater than great relief, I found a door that led to a place to poop. It had a sink too. I turned on the taps to make sure water was forthcoming. It did, but was not hot. A dispenser with antiviral goo stood on top of the poobowl. Eagerly I covered my hands and arms with the stuff and washed them clean. I would have ablushed more of my bod, except there was no dryingsheet, so I wiped my damp flesh upon my tunic before returning to the others.

Elijah had recovered. He sat next to Lilith, who held his hand in hers. She was saying something in a whisper. He nodded his head a few times. She stopped abrupt-like when she saw me enter, and let go. "Goodly news and bad," I said then perched my bot on the edge of the glass-topped short legged table. "No shower, but thank all and sundry, there is a wastebowl and sink with some sanitising gel." Lilith let her mouth rise up a bit at each corner.

Elijah stood. "I must go to that place at once. I have a feeling of knots and scurrying insects inside my innards. I need most urgently to rid my system of them."

"It is behind a door in the hallway opposite the one we came in. If you make too much of a pong, I have a scent spray." I pulled an atomiser from my other pant pocket. He took it from me and went swiftly to the talked about place. When he was quite gone, I turned my attentions to Lilith.

"Do not attempt to deceive me. Elijah has dropped you and yours in it and no mistake. What occurred today was not a spur of the moment thing."

"I have no idea."

"Let rip with the info or…"

"Or what?"

"I will not give you any grub."

"That is no concern to me. I have fasted

for longer than this."

"Fine, then I will deny Elijah also."

"He will not protest either. We are used to suffering for our religion."

"Which is all but banned in Cityplace."

"Which is why we must resort to underhand means to survive."

I had no argument at that moment, for truth be told, I did not have a clue why their religion should be denied. Granted Daniel seemed somewhat extreme, but from what I learned from schooling and vidinfo, they seemed goodly, kind folk that merely wished to live a life similar to that of their prophet. Elijah entered looking pale. He held out my scentspray. I took it from his shaking hand. Swallowing hard, he sat next to Lilith.

"There is water in the grub box, I will get some for you," I said and did just that. He snatched the bottle from my hand and drank in long gulps. "Erm, you might want to slow down a tad, if you are dehydrated, small sips would be advisable."

I had no sooner said those words when Elijah went a shade of green I had not seen before, and barfed most forcefully onto the whitewashed stone floor. I was grateful that he missed splattering me with his yellow bile, and quickly took several Cleanwipes from my pocket. With one hand pinching my nose, I wiped up the offending spew, raced into the pooplace, threw it down the bowl, and flushed it away. I gagged several times before washing my hands.

When I returned to the communal room, Elijah was lying flat on the cosycouch, his head resting on Lilith's thighs. She stroked his matted brown hair. I swear I saw a look of utmost tenderness in her eyes. She lifted her head when I entered and said, "He needs food and rest. If you will give him some nourishment then I will give you info in return."

Sly all right. Nodding, I searched the box for something comforting and found a sachet of self-heating lentil soup. I took a cling-wrapped bowl and spoon from a shelf above the recliner, opened the wrapper and handed the dish to Lilith. I shook the bag for a few secs until the blue indicator tab turned red, then pulled it open and poured it into the bowl.

"Thanks, Adara. May the Lord shine upon your soul." She nudged Elijah and with my helping hands, he sat upright. Lilith gently spooned the liquid into his mouth. I warned her of the dangers of feeding him too much all in one go.

"Perhaps you could finish the meal. We cannot let food go to waste." Lilith smiled and ate the rest.

Elijah gained colour to his cheeks and slowly stood. He stretched and yawned. I noticed that his face had lost its look of desperate. Underneath the muck and stubble, I fancied he might be somewhat fetching in appearance. I think I must have gawped too long for he furrowed his brow. I quickly turned away. Lilith licked the bowl and spoon dry then patted her newly rounded tum. I was amazed at how such a small portion of food could have such a dramatic effect, but then they were all but starved and any titbit would be of value.

"Thanks and more for the food Adara. Would I be able to use a room to rest in?"

"There are four all of the same design, pick any you wish. Oh, I have to ask Elijah, you will not try to escape will you?"

"How?"

"Well, you could attempt to break down the doors and flee that way."

Both Lilith and Elijah let forth a mighty guffaw. He rolled up the sleeves of his tunic and laid bare his scrawny arms. "I believe I would not be able to break a twig with these muscle-lacking arms let alone smash a large wooden door."

"Point taken. Go sleep. Do you wish to retire also Lilith?"

"Soon. I must first honour the promise I made earlier. Sleep well in peace Elijah."

"I think I will. Despite this prison and not knowing what is to become of us, I am all weary. Praisebee Cheseus."

"Praisebee his name."

They looked to me. "Erm yep, Praisebee the Cheesus." Elijah nodded to us both and left.

"I am loathed to give over the info you require. It goes against all that I believe and have vowed to do, but I must keep my word."

"That you must, but I feel a-grieved at being the cause of your conflict."

Lilith placed the empty bowl upon the table and put her elbows on her knees. She cupped her face in her hands. "Our order have been travelling for many years. There is unrest amongst us. Our faith is wavering. Daniel saw this and decided we needed to find a place to settle. But who would let us in?"

"No one I fear, your kind are not well regarded as far I can tell."

"Just so. There was a time just after the

Great Famine when disease brought about the near end of all hominids and animals, that Cityplace was built. A fortress to protect what remained of folk and keep out any lingering threat of pestilence."

"Yep, all this I know, get to the point."

"So be it. When this great metropolis was constructed, our kind outnumbered all else in settling here. Then greed ensued and those that did not abide by the strict hygiene laws, or the rigid philosophy of the OneGreatProvider that stated: 'Keep behind the fence. Stay within reach. Wash. Stay clean. Procreate. Survive,' were cast out."

"Nah, your story of history events are clouded by anger. We are taught in class that you Praisebees got all greedy and demanded the best of everything. That you wanted the rest to subscribe to your faith and do the bidding of the god the other folk deemed long dead, having abandoned his flock."

Lilith's face darkened. Her eyes seemed to glow with what can only be described as hate. "I will not argue semantics with a kiddle from a place that excludes those who need aid for fear of contamination. You may live in sterile bliss, but know nowt of the world that surrounds you. Little wonder you succumbed to the Agro sweetener and turned your backs and minds to their rising power. Just so long as you all had food."

I wanted to reply to her harsh words, but to be truthful, some of them pierced through my lack of giving a huff about anything other than my own problems. It was true when Cityplace was founded, or so we are told, that some did rebel and leave, such as the Woodsfolk tribe, but the Praisebees have always been the baddies, after the Carnies and Agros of course. My noggin was all jumbled. I wanted the convo to end. "You talk of long past times, the now is what we must concern ourselves about."

She folded her arms and leant back. It was an unnerving gesture that I found hostile. I decided to mimic her pose. She snorted. "Then let us concentrate on the moment, or as near to as is appropriate, to end my telling of how things came to pass. We have been camped in the Wilderness for some months now and have lost three 'dults to Wolfies."

"Nah, not Wolfies? Yeuk. Gruesome and then some."

"It was, but that was not the worst. Our hunger drove some to seek out Carnies. When they returned nothing was the same. Restlessness and doubt swamped us. Made some quite mad. Worse still, two little 'uns disappeared just four days ago. Since then all is fear and dread. We almost disbanded, but Daniel is good and strong. he told us that he received word from God that we were to settle in Cityplace and make it our home."

"Not likely for sure. The place is a fortress and no one gets in or out without prior knowledge. Even the Carnieval is monitored most severely, and those brutes only allowed in if escorted by City S.A.N.T.S."

"Exactly. So we decided to storm the place. We procured some weapons from a Woodsfolk that found our lair. In exchange, we gave him what little food we had. Then word came to us of the ghosties. It seemed the perfect opportunity to get in."

"Wow, some plan. Pity it didn't succeed, for you and yours, not ours of course."

Lilith smirked. "Tell me something, Adara?"

"Anything, if I can."

"Can you really bring the birdybirds down?"

"Not too certain about that. I know I can lure the raptors." I showed her the talon scars on my forearms and back of the neck. "Haven't quite got the right frequency to attract the smaller sort, and not quite honed my skill to avoid being gouged a bit."

"Quite a gift. With such a talent, you will be much in demand."

"Against my will. I have no desire to hurt said creatures just to satisfy the excess greed of Carnies and the like."

Lilith bit her lip and I swear I saw the same fire as before light up in her eyes.

## Chapter Nine
*Bundled Off To Who Knows Where*


I put my hand inside my tunic pocket and let my fingers rest on the hilt of the knife Orva gave me. Lilith stood. I did too.

"I shall rest. Again many thanks for the food much needed."

"Thanks for the info. Not sure what I'll do with it. Not sure it matters now that your lot are under the power of the Longarms."

"Who knows that we still are? When we left there was much chaos."

"That is true."

Lilith bowed a little and left. The hairs on the back of my neck stuck out when she passed by me. There was something about her that I did not trust. I tiptoed into the hallway and pressed my ear to the first closed door. Not a sound except for heavy breathing, that I guessed came from Elijah.

Softly, I footed my way to the pooplace. The door was open but the one next to it was not. I opened it and saw Lilith sitting on the bed, hunched over, gnawing on something fleshy. She lifted her head. I saw a glob of drool on her chin. She quickly wiped her face and tucked what she was eating into a soft brown pouch.

"Adara, can I be of use?"

"Nope, didn't realise you were in here. I came to lie down myself. This was the room I chose when first we entered."

She rose and headed for the door. "So sorry, I didn't realise you had picked this one for yourself. I shall leave."

"Nah, you can have it. I'll take the one opposite. Besides, there is a strange smell in here that I find unpleasant." I turned to leave, but swivelled round just before I reached the exit. "So, what were you consuming when I first came in?"

"Nothing."

I folded my arms and cocked my head to one side. She lowered her lids for a brief sec then looked at me all sweet of smile.

"Yes. I suppose I was eating something, of course. It is merely a root that I dug up in the Wilderness. I am ashamed at keeping it all for myself given Elijah's condition. But, it is a hard, glutinous thing. Had I offered him some, he would have expelled it in much the same way he did the water."

I narrowed my eyes and nodded. "Oh, right. It did indeed look strange to me when I saw it. What kind of root did you say it was?"

"I did not, for, in truth, I do not know what it is."

"Really? Strange that you should eat a thing that may be poisonous."

"Oh, it is not at all dangerous. I witnessed a Wolfie chomping on a similar thing."

"I'm sure you did," I said and left her to munch upon what could only be gristle and bone. I shuddered at the thought that Lilith was a Carnie. I attempted to dismiss such a notion from my nonce, but the evidence was too strong. I plodded off to my restingroom wondering how many more of the Praisebees ate meat.

I lay on the not so soft bed and closed my peepholes. Images of birdybirds being ripped limb from limb filled my head. I sat up 'bruptly. The idea that I had to stay in this confined place with Lilith and her loathsome weakness filled me with dread. I reached into my trouser pocket and pulled out the comdevice. My fingers hovered over the 'on' button. Then I put it back, went into the hallway, and walked down the passage to the door Dreng had locked. I pushed it, pulled it and kicked it hard, but it did not budge. Neither they nor I could hope to escape from that source.

With a yawn, for I was indeed fatigued

from all that had passed, I ambled back to the communal room. I rifled through the grub box for something sweet. Pulling out a grainbar, I plonked myself on the cosycouch and crunched down on the tasty sweet. The not so distant memory of Lilith and her gristle-chomping made me shiver. I looked to the hallway and vowed not to sleep. If Lilith could ingest dead meat of who knows what, then it would not be beyond the realms of feasibility that she could have notions of consuming my tender, living flesh. I dismissed the idea of her eating Elijah, not much on his bones to satisfy a Carnie.

Not knowing how long it would be before the S.A.N.T.S. returned, I searched the room for some sort of diversion to help me keep awake. To my delight, I found a playslab on the shelf above the one where I took the grubbox. I sat back down, turned it on and spent some time playing my favourite game of 'kittle-go-pounce'.

Although an enjoyable pastime, I could not concentrate. Soon my thoughts returned to what had occurred earlier. Now that all knew I had the gift, my life would not be my own. A realisation came to me. I would not be able to join S.A.N.T. camp. I groaned out loud. The noise must have woken Elijah, for within a few secs he was standing in the doorway rubbing his sleep-encrusted eyes.

"Are you ill? I heard moaning."

"Me? Nah, not me, never get sick. I was just expressing the hopelessness I feel. I made a mistake. Now must accept the consequences."

Elijah nodded, yawned, stretched, then sat upon the chair. That was when I saw his feet. Yeuk and then some. Grey muck stuck to the soles and heels. Bits of leaves and grass where embedded between his toes and as for the nails? They were as black and soil filled as a newly dug hole. Despite my revulsion, I could not turn my head away. Elijah noticed where my stare landed and bent forward. Looking down at his feet, he giggled. "Sandals do not keep out the grime of the forest floor I'm afraid. There are no places of ablution where we settled."

"How did you wash?"

"A quickly dip in the river once a week. Not so bad when the weather is warm, but when it is not, trips to said water are less frequent."

"It is a shame that there is no steamshower here. I would venture you would be pleased to stand beneath one."

"That I would. It has been many months since I have felt the warmth and deeply cleansing of such a luxury."

He gave out a sigh and smacked his lips. I took his actions to infer that he was still empty-bellied, so went to the grubbox for more food. I took out a packet of ricebread and held it out. "Would you care for some?"

"I would indeed, if it can be spared. In fact, as I am little unwell, perhaps I will partake of just a small amount."

Opening the wrapper, I gave him half, then sat back down and ate the rest. Elijah munched slowly. "Help yourself to more water. These roundels have a tendency to stick." He gulped, reached over to the box and extracted a small tube of water. He drank in tiny sips, took another bite of the disc then put the rest on his thigh.

"Are you no longer hungry?"

"I could consume the rest, but I will save some for Lilith. We must conserve our rations.

Not knowing if he was in on all this Carnie stuff, I was unsure whether to tell him of what I saw in Lilith's restroom. Tapping my fingers on the arm of the couch, I said in quite a throw away manner, "Elijah, have you ever eaten meat?"

"What? No, never. I have no desire to."

I continued my interrogation by leaning forward, resting my chin upon my knuckles and squinting with one eye. "Have you ever witnessed any of your flock consuming such food stuffs?"

Elijah furrowed his brow and passed his fingers through his mud-caked, dark hair. He lowered his eyes for a sec then stared at me. "I did once. It was several weeks ago, when a Wolfie took the first of us. The beast left behind some stray bits of innards and the like. We were hungry in the extreme, spring was late in coming. There was little to forage or steal out in the edge of the Wilderness. It was before we befriended a Woodsfolk and had only a sack or two of grain left. I was getting firewood and heard a most unpleasant slurping sound. I thought it was the Wolfie returning to consume what it had dropped, but when I peeked around the tree I was hiding behind, I saw one of our own chewing on a piece of offal."

I did not react to his words, instead, I simply said, "Go ahead, finish your food, Lilith is not hungry." He bent his head, sighed and ate. There was more to this Lilith fem than she would have us all believe. A Carnie for sure, and resourceful. It was she who freed Elijah, but not Daniel. Oddly indeed. Elijah drained his water tube and rose.

"I will rest again. There is no telling what will take place from here-on-in. Will you not to bed?"

"Nah, have a bad case of the jitters for some reason. Can't seem to settle."

He smiled thinly and left. I wondered how long before we would be free of this strange place, hoped it would be soon. I went to the pooproom and relieved myself. Then did it again. Nerves. Not surprising I suppose, but not nice. I rinsed my hands, shook off the excess liquid, went back into the communal room and flopped onto the cosycouch. Tiredness washed over me. I let my head loll back, vowing to close my eyes for no more than a sec.

"Adara, wake."

I felt a hand gently rock my shoulder and opened my eyes. Orva knelt in front of me. "We must leave. Come quickly and quietly. We must not awaken the others."

"What? Are they not coming too?"

"No, not yet. Not until we have figured out what to do with them."

"But Elijah is unwell. There is not so much grub and Lilith…"

"Do not concern yourself with the fate of these two insurgents."

"Elijah is not like that, he is good and kind. Also, I think he is in danger."

"From whom?"

"Lilith."

"I think not. She freed only him. Therefore, she is more fond of him than you would like."

That I could not argue with. I stood and Orva placed two grubboxes onto the floor.

"I have brought more provisions. They will be fine for many moons to come." Orva gestured for me to go to the exit, I hesitated and she all but dragged my limp bod to it. She took a swift look back then pushed me through.

## Chapter Ten
*Another Place Of Hiding*

This corridor was wide and brightly lit by one long fluorescent light tube that stretched all the way along the ceiling. Grey and cold, it stretched a goodly way. "Keep moving until you get to a black door," Orva said.

In the distance, a dark oblong shape came into view. I ran swiftly towards it. It was huge. Big enough for a whole tree to go through. "Why is it so vast?"

"I have no idea, perhaps whoever built it had something in mind. Perhaps they needed it to be large so that they could get large things through," she said and looked at me as though I was a bub. She knocked twice, then three times on the door and I heard the same sequence tapped back. Orva took a big metal key from her backpack, inserted it into the lock and turned. The door made a heavy clunking sound as it opened. I strained my neck in an attempt to see what was beyond it.

"Stay close to me. Follow each step I take as if you were my shadow."

We stepped out into semi-darkness. I sucked in outside air and coughed. Dreng stood before us and put his finger to his lips. Orva tilted her head to the moonless sky, sniffed, then motioned for us to follow. I did what she told me, mimicking her quick strides.

It was hard to keep up, at first, her legs being longer than mine, but I managed without too much loss of breath. Although I was disorientated and had no clue where we traipsed, the familiar high-up search lights that ringed the perimeter fence, blasted on and I calmed as we moved past less shady objects I recognised. As the dimness faded I realised that we were at the outer edges of Cityplace.

The dazzling lights that lit the sky and made the stars run for cover, came closer into view. We stopped.

"Cams and Flashlighters are everywhere. The whole place is on alert looking for you. That Daniel male blabbed about the exit we took. Now all strive to find the portal. Although it is well hidden and impossible to open, they are aware of its existence. Who knows, perhaps some Meek may stumble on its unlocking device."

"Where to now?"

Dreng stepped forward and said in a loud whisper, "To a secret S.A.N.T. safe place. Ye will be secure there for sure."

Orva pointed to a large container. It was one of the many huge waste bins that flanked the outer perimeter of Cityplace. No one but the Sanitary cleaners were allowed access to them. Although, once when playing, 'hide-and-I'll-go-seek' with Santy Breanna, Deogol and I hid behind one. She found us super quick of course and gave us such a scolding that we never went back.

"It is a basic hideaway."

"What, more basic than the underground thingy?"

"Afraid so. But, there is a vidscreen and companel for us to communicate."

"No steamshower?"

"No."

"A pooplace at least?"

"Well, there is an organicwastebox."

"I will have to relieve myself in a thing that does not flush?"

"Indeed. But it is hygienic in its own way."

I pressed my head against the sticky outer surface of the container and let out a lengthy groan.

"Ah, come on now, ye will adapt, ye are S.A.N.T. trained."

"Only partially, I have not yet gone to

camp."

"Ye will thrive, I know it."

I pulled away and wiped the sludgy stuff from my forehead. I did ask once what the containers were made from. Santy had no clue and merely said, "They are fashioned from the stuff they are fashioned from. Best not to wonder at things that are of little concern."

Orva lay flat on her back and shuffled herself underneath the vastly box. Then reached up and twiddled something. A small flap flipped open and hung down. "This is how you enter and leave. Come follow me inside." She pulled herself up and out of sight. I sank to the floor, as Orva had, and wriggled my way through the gap; which was indeed a tight fit.

The interior of the wastebin was a large cylindrical space that boasted nowt more than a small bed against one of the walls, two wooden chairs, a round wooden table in the centre, and a shelf opposite the bed that had a companel and vidscreen upon it.

It was illuminated by a series of small oblong light strips stuck to the ceiling that gave off a harsh white light and made the sound of an angry bumble. At the far end was the dreaded organicwastebox. In full view, not even behind a screen. I bit my lip and tried not to show my utter disappointment at the gloomy surroundings. Orva slapped me on the back. "Don't look so glum. It's not as bad as it looks. There are soft blankies to keep you warm. Stacks of provisions. Games enough to amuse you during your stay."

"Which will not be long I trust?"

"We are doing everything we can to argue your case. We are close to them agreeing to go to trial."

"What? But I'm no Crim."

"We know that, but in order for you to live how you wish, laws must be written and old ways amended. That means…"

"A long drawn out legal battle."

"Let us hope not so long."

"Cheer up Adara, yer Santy is quite a talker and so to yer Greatgrangran."

I groaned even louder than before. "No not her, she was the one that blabbed."

"Aye, she is right sorry too. She will prevail, she has a quick and learned mind."

"Now we must leave. The com device I gave you will not work so well inside this storage place. The materials used to make it are of an unusual mix. Signals can penetrate going in but not out. You cannot call us but we can speak to you."

"Do nay look so forlorn, ye will be well."

I sloped off to the not so comfy bed, lay down, and threw my arms across my face. For some reason, an image of Deogol flashed in front of my eyes. I sat up. "Where is Deogol?"

Orva and Dreng looked at one another, then at the floor. I stood. My innards flipped flopped. I felt a coldness grip my chest.

"Where is my bro?"

"Best if your Santy speaks to you of that. Truly Adara it is not our place. We are to keep you safe, please ask no more from us," Orva said. She took off her backpack, rummaged around inside and took out several small objects. "Dreng, will you wait for me without?"

He nodded, gave me a cheerful face and left. When he was gone Orva walked to the table and plonked the stuff she retrieved from her bag onto it.

"Adara, let your expression lighten. Think not of your bro at this time."

"How can I not when you are so evasive with info about his safety?"

"There was concern for him, but he is in no danger, that much I can relate."

The rigidness in my shoulders relaxed. I

sat upon one of the hard wooden chairs. Orva sat opposite me and waved her hand across the things strewn on the table before us. "I have left you some more personal supplies. Only as a precaution in case your stay here is for longer than anticipated. Some means of sanitising yourself with these Steriwipes, and Stayfresh cloths."

Leaning forward, I saw amongst the cleaning stuff more intimate provisions for when the moon pulled upon my womb. A time fast approaching and a thing forgot in all the turmoil. I warmed to Orva and her thoughtfulness. Despite her muscular frame, short hair and lack of facial enhancements, I realised she was just as much a fem as myself. I smiled and she returned my gift with one of her own, then rose. "I too must leave you. Try to rest." A beeping noise came from the comdevice. "Ah, I think that may be your Santy. Sleep well Adara," she said, went through the hatch and closed it.

I picked up the portacom, clicked the on the speaker button and said, "Santy, where is Deogol?"

Her voice was calm. I clenched my eyes tight and wished that I were at home. "He is in his room. Now, that is. When all the fuss died down, I returned, he was gone. Caused quite a panic. Who told you he went missing? Orva?"

"Nah, I just had a feeling. Is he well?"

"As ever, but, even more broody and withdrawn than before. He refuses to tell where and with whom he has been with. He didn't even ask about your welfare."

"He has something going on I think."

"For sure. I have forbade him to go outside."

"Yeah, right, like that is a punishment."

"It would seem to be on this occasion, for when I said those words he became most vocal and threw his food at the wall."

"Strange behaviour."

"It is indeed, but you must not fret. Greatgrangran and I are to visit the council just after sunup. We will have you home by noon."

"You sound most sure."

"Adara, the folk reacted unreasonably, they know that. I believe they are sincerely ashamed. Besides, they have the Praisebees and perhaps Carnievale to think of. Odd noises and light flashes have been heard and seen without."

"What has become of the Praisebees?" I said, becoming less concerned about my drab environment and more interested in their fate.

"I heard that they are being held in the Decontamination place. Seemed appropriate. Did you see their feet?"

A vivid image of Elijah's filthy toenails entered my noggin. I near retched at the memory of it. "I did. Gruesome. What of the two that escaped with me?"

"What two? I did not know of this?"

I closed my mouth and heard Santy ask if I was still there. I said I was and there came a long pause. "Where are they, Adara?"

"That you must ask Orva and Dreng."

"Oh, I will."

"Santy?"

"Yes?"

"The male juve Praisebee, he is ill. I do not think he is like the others. But the fem, she is I believe, a Carnie. Most of the other one's too I think. I saw bits of fleshy stuff in their teeth when they let forth with their wailings. I cannot be certain sure, but the Lilith one is. I swear I saw her nibbling on something that resembled a bone, when she thought she was alone."

"Info duly noted." Santy's voice lost its gentleness and if I were sitting across the eating table at home, I would see her face darken and her mouth turn downwards. "I must say goodlynightly to you now. When the meeting is done I will convey what went on."

"Santy?"

"Yes?"

"Air kiss Deogol for me."

"I will, and do the same to you."

I switched off the comdevice and put my head in my hands. So much had occurred that I could not rightly get to grips with any of it. I was befuddled indeed.

Images of blood encrusted Prasiebees screaming and shouting swirled inside my skull. Then the face of Elijah, wan and skeletal filled my noggin until I thought it would burst. I stood, but came over faint, so put my hand upon the back of the chair to steady myself. I found it difficult to breathe. For an instant, I saw the space closing in on me. With the walls moving ever nearer and the ceiling rushing down. I crouched on the floor and let my lungs empty in the form of a scream.

## Chapter Eleven
*Everything Changes*

There was drool in the corner of my mouth and my neck was stiff. I rolled onto my back and felt the cold of the not-really-metal-or-plastic floor, seep into my flesh. I shivered, rubbed my arms to promote circulation, then stood.

The bright buzzing lights hurt my eyes and my stomach yearned for food. With a yawn I stretched. Then said, "Ow," as my muscles clicked.

I went to the organicwastebox, lifted the lid and peered inside. There was a gloopy looking brown liquid in the bottom that smelled like autumn leaves.

Despite being quite alone, I still found it difficult to do my bowel movements in the open. I longed for a door to hide me, and for a sweet-smelling bumwipe to cleanse said bot. Much had occurred to make me toughen up, so I told myself that I was at home in the hope it would get my innards going. To my great relief, it worked.

Nad. I forgot to grab a wipe from the table. With my pants around my ankles, I tottered over to it, and took a handful of cleaning cloths. Thoroughly cleansed of all traces of poop, I threw the soiled wipes into the wastebox. I looked for a handle by which to engage the flushing action. There was nowt except for a sign saying, 'Place all soiled items into the bowl. Close the lid'. I did and hoped the smell that hovered above my head would soon dissipate.

I ambled back to the table and picked up several scented swabs. These I used to clean areas of my bod that were given over to stinkiness. Then I rifled through the grubbox for something to eat. I found some self-heating porridge, pulled out the activation tab, waited for the small yellow patch at the side to turn red, then supped it down, straight from the package. I longed to be free of this gloomy place and wondered if the sun had risen. Or the moon, having no notion of what part of the day or night it was.

This made me agitated once more. I took in some long breaths and searched the chamber for the source of fresh air. I slid my hands across the walls, which were smooth, not slimy like they were on the outside, and felt tiny holes all over. My nose touched the surface. Yep, I had to be that close to actually see the minute apertures that punctured the entire surface. No wonder it was cold. Still, a cunning way of aerating the place. I pressed my eye to an opening, but it was too small. All I saw was the outline of my lashes.

My feet hurt from the lack of warmth, so I jumped on the spot to create heat. It did the trick. I took to jogging around the space to give me something to do other than worry. Besides, I missed the ritual of running up the stairs to our home.

When I was out of breath, and to my dismay, all sweaty, I lay on the bed. My thoughts turned to the fate of Elijah and Lilith. Why did Orva and Dreng not tell Santy about them? A thought occurred to me that they meant to leave them in the room to starve. I sat upright and forced my mind to think of less unpleasant things. It didn't work, so I resorted to amusing myself by playing the vidgames that lay on the shelf.

They were old in design, basic in graphics and were not up to the standard I was used to. One was a sort of puppet show of a fave ancient play show. Aamlet Prince of the Great Dane. Dramdram was the only lesson I paid attention to in class. I don't know why I favoured the shouty male and his grief-filled procrastinations, but I did. The visuals were dodgy, though, so I went back to the game thingy's instead. They made a pleasing sound. Some even had tunes I recognised. I sang along with them and became less a-feared.

One of the distractions was a cartoony-style kiddles sport called, 'Birdyseek'. Although quite lame, it had the most realistic birdybirdy sounds. I let the thing run on and on, listening to the many different twitterings. Trying to filter out the singsonginess in order to concentrate on what they all had in common, such as pitch and inflection. When I thought I had located a recurrent tweet, I began to mimic it. Thusly preoccupied, I practised for quite some secs until I believed I had mastered the tunefulness and modulation. So, that was why the birdies did not come before. I was singing the wrong song.

I strode around the room and let rip loud and clear. If I had been outside I dare say flocks of birdles would have descended. Closing my eyes, I imagined myself in a field with flowers, butterflies, and birdybirds perched upon my shoulders. Not that I'd ever been in an actual field, all this memorypic stuff came from downloads on the vidcomp.

The portacom beeped. I opened my lids right quick then raced over to it. I clicked it on. Santy's voice! "Goodly news indeed. They have come to a compromise regarding your talent. Which I explained was not developed beyond the embryonic stage. Greatgran Amranwen presented your case with gusto, and even managed to get them to agree for you to attend S.A.N.T. camp when you are of age."

I shouted with much glee, "So, I can come home?"

"Indeed, you can. However, there is one thing, though, a condition that I had to agree to. The alternative was Decontamination."

I gulped. "What is the condition?"

"That you practice your skill for the gathering to honour the OneGreatProvider. They want you to bring some birdybirds for all to gaze upon."

"Nah, won't do that. Might turn into a massacre of the little things. What with the Carnies lurking somewhere nearby."

"It is the one and only condition."

"I'm surprised you agreed."

"I told you the alternative. Do you relish the thought of being decontaminated? Do you forget how it was for Deogol?"

"No. But Santy, it is wrong for me to do

this. What if the sight of said birdles causes some folk to turn their thoughts towards the consumption of meat?"

"It is a risk to be sure. There are many who look back to the time before the Great famine and long for a taste of flesh. I have heard talk of those that have eaten it and would do so again. Perhaps, though, it may put folk's mind at rest. All of this subterfuge and hiding, it is no way to live. Your gift should be celebrated."

"But the Carnies. All know they are near. It may bring them forth eager and nasty."

"There is that. However, we will have the advantage if such a thing does occur. Perhaps it would be best if they were to be flushed out like that. Their nefarious ways only add to the fear, once outed they will seem less of a threat and will think twice before troubling us with their strange doings. Nowt good can come from their vile amusements."

"But…"

"It will be but the once. Really. I have been assured. Please agree so that you can come home."

There was a quivering in her voice and I knew that other matters pressed heavily upon her. Loath as I was to do such a thing, I had no choice. To be decontaminated was not something to relish. When they decided that Deogol was indeed a Meek, he was still just a kiddle, but they took him away to 'cure' his strange ways. When he came back, he was not the bro I remembered. To this day, he awakens with evil nightdreams about what was done to him. I put aside my horror and disgust. "I will do this, but I will not do it gladly."

"I am pleased that you have chosen to comply. I will come for you now."

"Will not Orva or Dreng release me?"

"No, they are attending to other matters, but will join us later. Ready yourself Addy."

"I will Santy, be sure of that." I switched off the comdevice. I looked at the stuff Orva had left and wondered if both she and Dreng were being punished in some way for keeping the Praisebees hostage in the cavern. But the fact that I was free again pushed back such wonderings. I waited most anxiously for Santy to come.

The wait was not long. Before the coldness could creep throughout my bod, I heard the hatch open. Santy Breanna stood before me. I ran to her and she bundled me up in her arms. I felt her warm, wet tears on my neck and pulled away. She wiped her eyes quickly. "Come let us go. I dare say you will glad to be rid of this confining and dreary place."

It was a sun-drenched day that greeted us when we dropped down from the container. I sucked in a lungful of air and gagged. There was an unpleasant smell not present when I went in. I thought it came from the wastebins, but they were sealed tight so no pong could escape. I raised my nose and sniffed.

"Ah yes, the smell. That would be the burning of the Praisebee's clothing. Sheriff Fychan thought it would be a moral booster to publicly incinerate their garments. A gesture to say that they are at the mercy of Citydwellers I dare say. Come let us slip back unnoticed. Addy, are you up to a slight diversion?"

With a nod, Santy bounded off in the direction of the border fence. I followed quickly and we came to a halt by one of the City perimeters. A guard dressed in a black all-in-one thwack proof uniform, waved his zapgun at us. Santy waved back and to my astonishment, walked straight past him, through an open gate, into the Wilderness.

Pausing for a sec, I blinked away some lingering sleep gunge, then joined her at the other side of the fence. She beckoned for me to come to her, then whispered into my ear, "We are to skirt round to the main entrance. This way no one will discover the S.A.N.T. hideout. Do not worry about the guards, they were S.A.N.T.S. once and were under my command before I left to care for you and your bro."

I turned my head and took in my first proper look at the Wilderness. Trees, bushes, brambles and all sorts of greenery growing wild, anywhere they liked. So different from the puny bits of verdure that struggled to survive in the bland, sterile atmosphere of Cityplace.

The smell in this abundant place was both sweet and pungent. I did not sneeze as I sucked in the damp leaf aroma. Feeling at home amongst the greenery, I fell to my knees to better sniff the rotting wood and musky fungus scents. Digging my mitts into the earth, I squeezed the soil between my fingers. Santy tapped me on the shoulder and handed me a wipe. I rose reluctantly and cleaned the cloying dirt from my tingling hands. "Santy, may we go deeper into this forest?"

"We must get back Addy, I am concerned for Deogol."

"Oh, right, yeah, sorry. Let us be swift then."

Santy ran on ahead and I kept up with her. For one of her advancing years, she was as quick as any juve I knew. She leapt over fallen twigs, sidestepping deep holes with such expertise, that I forgot she was my Santy for a sec and thought of her as the Backpacker she used to be. I made sure I stepped where she did for fear of tumbling upon something on the ground. I was not dressed for such a caper though and my feet began to throb. The shoes I wore were best suited for accessorising indoor garb, rather than being a buffer from the thorns and stones that littered the Wilderness's floor.

We pushed our way through some dense foliage. The outpost gate to the main City entrance came into view and we slowed our pace. Santy took a spyglass from her backpack. After looking through it for no more than a sec, she pinched her thumb and index finger together, put them in her mouth and blew. It was a piercing whistle that caused the border guard to turn his attention in our direction. Santy waved her arms in the air in a series of elaborate gestures and was answered by said guard making the same movements back. We walked stealthily to the gate, past the guard, who nodded his head. "Welcome back, Catcher of Birds."

Santy walked on ahead. The place was full of folk. They lined either side of the plaza as though awaiting some great event. When I came full into the square, a roar blasted from the crowd. Arms were raised and voices sang out my name, "Adara, Adara, Adara," they chanted and I clung to Santy Breanna not knowing what to make of such a spectacle.

## Chapter Twelve
*Treated Like Royalty*

Mayor Eldwyn, a short white-haired oldie, (one of the few ancients allowed to roam free and live out of the Goldenagehome complex) stepped forward and offered me his wrinkled hand. Santy unpeeled my fingers from around her waist and pushed me forward. I gave his mitt a goodly grip, then smiled a bit as he winced when I vigorously shook it. I let go and he rubbed his knuckles. "Adara, welcome back from wherever it was you have been. Since you are here, I assume your Santy has filled you in with our wishes?"

"Yep, but know that I do your bidding because I fear the consequences if I do not. I am unhappy with what you want me to do, for I am concerned it will ignite the urges in those who may be weak for a taste of flesh, but do it I will."

He leant forward. In a low hoarse voice he said, "I too am unhappy with the decision so have instructed all not to touch any of the birdles, should the chance occur." He stood upright and addressed the crowd, "Cityfolk, we have our beloved Adara back."

What? Since when have I been 'beloved'? I looked at the beaming crowd and could not believe that all smiles were for me. Even Drysi and Hypra gave me a friendly grin. My noggin swam with the strangeness of it all.

Mayor Eldwyn continued, "She has agreed to bring the birdies for all to see so that we may delight in their presence and bathe in the sweet twitterings that cheer the soul and mind. But be warned. Those who have a desire to indulge in fleshy cravings will be dealt with most severely. The ceremony is one of joy. A celebration of our endurance through great adversity. It may be that the gathering of the birdybirds will bring the Carnies slavering to our gates. But we are prepared and they shall not enter. Know that Adara will do this but the once, so do not attempt to harass her further. If any are found to be doing so, they will be placed in the filth hole for two moonrises."

There was a mass gasp.

"As for the Praisebees, well, they will be fairly judged and sentenced at sunup." A loud booing ensued followed by many mean words meant for Praisbee ears alone. "Adara shall spend her time until the praising day honing her skills and making ready."

"I will?"

"Indeed little fem, your Santy made us aware of your incompetence at said task. Also, your failed attempt that panicked so many is proof you need to refine your warblings."

I could not argue with him as I was inexperienced. I shrugged. He put his arm around my shoulders. "You will go without any fuss. A Lady is waiting for you. She will dress you for the occasion and groom you so you look your best. You will stay in the Authority Homes for that period of time. If you require any special treats, you need only ask, they shall be provided."

"What? I am to be primped by a Lady?" I'd heard of said fems. Although rumours abounded of their secret comings and goings around the wealthier parts of Cityplace, I did not know of anyone who had actually seen one in the flesh. My body reacted to the news with a full on sweat attack. I turned to Santy.

She shook her head then smiled. "You must comply with their wishes. I am as surprised as you at this turn of events. I would rather you were home with Deogol and me."

The mayor took my hand. "Come, do not

look so sad, you are to stay in the best accommodation in all of Cityplace. You shall be made into a fine Lady when said fem has finished with you."

I pulled myself free of his flimsy grip. "Nah, nope, nadder, no ta. It is my lifeplan to become a S.A.N.T. end of. If you were to give me an honest look, you would not even contemplate the notion of forcing me to be what I am not and cannot be." As soon as I uttered these words I remembered Deogol saying a similar thing when Santy suggested he join us on a camping trip. A feeling of dread filled my guts and I became unstable. Santy steadied me. I calmed enough to say, "That is that. Send the good Lady home."

Mayor Eldwyn scratched his thin hair. "So be it, Adara."

"Also, one more thing, may I please be allowed to go home?"

"Well, you have your Santy and other guards have been appointed, so, yes, you can return home."

I sighed a deep sigh of relief. Then again when I saw two familiar faces. The mayor greeted them with a wide grin. "Ah, here are your escorts Adara. I believe you have already met. They will attend to your needs and take you to the City borders where you shall spend your time practising your art. They will be your personal guards, so that none shall attempt to molest or abduct you whilst you work."

"Hi Orva, Dreng."

They nodded and stood either side of me.

A group of musicians stepped from the crowd. They played a sombre tune that made the crowd lower their heads. Several drums beat a slow rhythm, whilst violentins and fluttles rose and fell with almost tearful notes. After a few secs of this mournful melody, I found myself wiping away a spot of wet from the corner of my eye. A profound coughing and shuffling of feet was heard. Mayor Eldwyn raised his hands. They stopped. "Let us hear a jaunty song to play whilst Adara parades through our square to her home."

Ah no. I was to be put on display for all to see. Aware of my tattiness and lack of clean, I did not relish the prospect and turned to Santy Breanna. "Is there any way I can be spared this embarrassment?"

"I think not. All eyes are indeed on you Addy. Square your shoulders, lift your chin. Flaunt your imperfection. This is your day and no mistake. I will be right behind you."

She touched my cheek, frowned and

pulled a Steriwipe from her pocket. I took it, turned away from the throng so as to give my face a goodly wash. Santy patted down my unruly, short hair, then twiddled me round. Mayor Eldwyn waved to the assembled folk. "Make noise with your mouths, hands and feet, in praise of Adara - Catcher of Birds!"

A great roar rose from the crowd. This time, the musicians played a quick-time jig. The trumpets and fluttles sending forth high notes that quite frankly hurt my ears. The mayor took my hand and led me forward. The music faded as the drummer struck up a solemn beat. Santy stood to my right and Mayor Eldwyn gave me a slight push. "Go before the rabble riot."

I straightened my spine, threw back my shoulders and walked steadily through the plaza. The band followed, so too the crowd. All was a cacophony of discordant notes from instruments and voices. I wanted to put my hands over my lugholes to dampen the hideous din and leg it fast home, but knew I could not.

Orva and Dreng strode in front of me and pushed away the occasional folk that tried to touch my bod. How I became an icon so quickly was baffling. Not so long ago Drysi and Hrypa were humiliating me in front of one and all. Now? Now I was being cheered and revered. I strained my neck to see if any familiar faces were there. "Where is Greatgrangran?"

Santy leaned forward. "I have left her with Deogol. She is fierce when she wants to be. Easily able to keep him from going out and getting lost again."

"What? What is this about Deogol getting lost?"

"Never mind all that, carry on walking. I will fill you in with what's what when we are home." She stood straight and waved to the onlookers.

As I followed a humungous rapture-filled shrieking erupted. Huffin' hell, how folk can change and become as one when forced together. I became uneasy at the wild-eyed expressions on their faces and hurried my pace to keep up with the S.A.N.T.S. ahead. The mayor trotted up beside me. "Too many wanting to grab a piece of you. Good that you will be out of the plaza soon."

Orva and Dreng pushed a path through the gathered folk. I hurried through the gap. As I did, I felt many hands touch my arms and head. My heart pounded. I began to breathe all-quick like. When the crowd began to close in and paw at my clothes as if to rip pieces off by way of a souvenir, Santy whistled. Orva and Dreng whipped out a dispersal grenade and threw it into the air. The red disc twirled most rapidly before exploding with a loudly shriek.

The crowd moved away as the ear-piercing siren continued. Mayor Eldwyn, hands over his ears like the rest of us, nodded and walked rapidly in the direction of his top-notch accommodation in the swanky Authority Homes. A part of me regretted not taking him up on his offer of a stay in the grand place, but I yearned to see Deogol again. A thing I did not normally do, but I could not get an image of him out of my thoughts. Why I should be so antsi over my bro so suddenly, I could not tell. Santy, all squint of eye, chin gestured for me to carry on walking and I did, most quickly.

What a wonder the grenade was. The sound it emitted was so unpleasant that within a few secs my adoring public were nowhere to be seen. Finally, the horrible noise faded and I freed my lugholes of the fingers I'd inserted to quell the din. "Wow Santy, that is a powerful weapon."

"Indeed. Shame we have so few at our disposal. Once we could order them direct from the Agros, but no more. They have cut off all communication with S.A.N.T.S."

"What is their plan?"

"This we do not know."

I felt all squirmy inside and was glad to see the shinning shape of Puritytowers not too far in the distance. The sickly feel grew stronger. I grimaced at the fact the reddiness would soon be upon me.

## Chapter Thirteen
*Menace On The Wind*

The glass doors to Puritytowers whooshed open and dished out a friendly blast of disinfectant vapour as we stepped inside. I sneezed. Before the snot formed into a drop on the end of my snout, Santy swiped it off with a sterile wipe. She handed me another, just in case, and threw the soiled one into the refuse funnel at the side of the entrance. It sucked it out of her hand and made a gurgle sloop noise as the thing went down to who knows where.

"Ta."

"You look tired and hungry. Perhaps we should refrain from our usual. Let us take the lift."

"Nah, no way, I'm taking the stairs. You two want a race?" I said to Dreng and Orva. They looked to Santy, who nodded. "Goodly good. Will you count us down?"

"Most willingly. One, two, three," Santy said. On hearing the last digit, I near flew to the grand stairs that led to our abode, and leapt up them two steps at a time.

"Try harder."

I turned my head to the left and saw

Dreng speed past me.

"Much harder."

I turned to the right and watched all breathless and in amazement as Orva raced up the stairs, overtaking Dreng as she went. Nad. They were good. I soon reached the top where Santy also stood. How did she manage to get to the outside stairs and onto the landing before me? "What the huff Santy? Are you made of different stuff than the rest of us?"

She smirked and pointed at the lift. "Took the elevator."

"Shifty."

"No, just getting past my prime."

"Never, Breanna," Dreng said and gave her a look that would have made me blush.

Orva coughed. "Are we to stay out here?"

"No, no, come, let us go to our abode. It is not so large. For the time being, you are to stay with us, we will need to double up on sleeping arrangements."

What? Now that was something I had not bargained for. "Will I have to share with Deogol?"

"Ah, that would be inadvisable the way you both squabble over the least little thing."

"Choc and the eating of it is no little thing, Santy."

"Perhaps, but to get so violent is not goodly Adara. Your poor bro will be scarred for life."

"Pah! 'Twas but a flesh wound."

"Indeed it was, a deeply one."

I would have argued more, but we reached our home, the time for quarrel was done. Santy slipped the unlockcard along the entrance slit and the door opened. We entered with another blast of cleansing mist and heard raised voices, accompanied by much clanging of metal things on cooking surfaces.

"It would seem, that Greatgran is having trouble with your bro."

We trundled down the bright corridor into the kinsfolk room. Santy gestured for Orva and Dreng to sit. They did and we went straight into the small foodprep place where Deogol sat all stiff-like at the table. His arms were folded, his head turned away from Greatgrangran, who was pushing a bowl of something gooey across the surface.

"You will eat what is presented before you, young 'un."

"No, I will not. Santy lets me eat choc if I want, when I want. She never forces me to munch on stuff that is kept at the back of the food cupboard for a good reason."

"What a whopper," I said. Deogol near fell from his chair.

Greatgrangran put her hand to her mouth and snickered. Santy shook her head. My bro lowered his. He stared at the table top as though his eyes would blast through the thing and allow him to make a hasty escape from his embarrassment.

"I knew you were fibbing, little earwig. I may be old-old, but I am not addled. Adele, glad you are home all safe." Greatgrangran looked over my shoulder. "I see you have brought visitors."

"That I have. S.A.N.T. guards to protect Adara."

"From what?"

My bro looked up.

"From the folk that wish to grab her and use her skills. The mayor will have her bring the birdles for the OneGreatProvider day. I told you this before I left."

Greatgrangran scratched her nose and pouted her saggy mouth. "Did you now? Well, I must not have heard you."

"That would be right." Deogol turned to us. "All she does is sit on the comfycouch and play on her slab. When I do such stuff I am admonished."

I near applauded my bro for using such a

big word, but Santy frowned. I said nowt.

"Greatgrangran is old and has served our community well. If, in the last great part of her life, she chooses to amuse herself with comp games, then so be it, she is entitled. You are not."

The argument lost its fire when Orva entered. "Sorry, 'scuse the interruption, but we have orders to take Adara to practise her vocal skills. The ceremony is but a few moons away."

I looked down at my dirty outfit. "I need to wash and put on fresh garments."

Santy relaxed her stiff-shouldered stance, gave Deogol a 'Don't you dare say anything' look and put her hand on my shoulder.

"Indeed you do. Whilst we are all here, I must re-arrange our sleeping quarters so as to fit in our guests."

Deogol snorted. "I'll not give up my room. I need quiet and solitude for my studies."

"What studies are you taking outside of class?"

My bro shuffled in his chair, then went the colour of the sky at sunrise. "Extra stuff that they do not teach."

"Like what?" Santy said. She bent low, put her elbows on the table and leant in close to Deogol.

"Stuff, just stuff, okay!" He pushed back his chair and stood. His face reddened even more. I thought he was about to blub when Grangran touched his arm.

"Leave the lad be. He has much to occupy his mind it would seem. Who are we to deny him this?"

Santy slowly straightened and took a long breath. "This matter will keep. Deogol, worry not, you will not need to give up your room, however, you will need to share it."

"Not with Adara!"

"Oy, no need to sound so mean," I said, more hurt than I should have been.

"Calm, calm. No, you will not share with your sister, but with Dreng. Worry not, for he will be guarding Adara during the moontime when you should be asleep. He will rest during your waking hours. Do not show me that face. It is done."

My bro scowled, clenched his hands, but did not respond. Santy nodded. "Orva and I will share. You can remain as is, Adara. Before you say another word, Deogol, your sister is of an age when she needs alone time and space to become who she is. This arrangement will be brief. Now, go wash and change. You must rehearse before the light diminishes."

"Rightly so. Back in a few secs," I said and went to my room.

Once inside I became heavy of limb and longed to lie down, but I could not, so went straight to the cleansing place. I secured the door, not knowing rightly why, and took off my smelly clothes. Then I threw them into the wallbasket, stepped into the glass-fronted cubicle and let the steamshower jets blast away all trace of sweat, muck and slime. Then I dried myself on a fluffly towel and went back into my sleeping quarters to choose suitable attire for my practise.

I opened the clothespace and pulled out my favourite outside troos made from thick, brown synthowool, and a black, long-sleeved tunic. Baggy enough to allow me to stretch and belt out my song. With a wink to my animal murals, I placed said garments on the chair by the window, then took out suitable undergarments from the beddrawer.

The bazoomiecups felt tighter than before. Yep, for sure my mams were swelling and becoming sore. Which meant only one thing, that the reddiness was fast approaching. I dressed quickly and went back to the kinsfolk room.

All were snuggled up close, resting on the

comfycouch, except for Greatgrangran. She was sitting on the big chair playing some game thingy on her slab. Santy stood in the doorway of the eating place and chewed on her fingernail. My bro sat hunched up in between Orva and Dreng, who stared at the wall as if it were showing an interesting vid.

"Hi-hi. I am all changed."

At the sound of my voice, and quick as a Curfewrebel clocked by a Flashlighter, both S.A.N.T.S. poinged up from their seats. "If you are ready we must go."

"Yeah, in a sec, Orva. I was wondering if I might not partake of some grub first?"

"Ye must practice before curfew. Ye will come now, eat later," Dreng said and waved his large mitt towards the door.

"I will, for sure. I just need something to munch on."

"If you must. Select something suitable to be consumed on the move. We are to take you to where you will…"

"Practice, I know. Fine, I'll do that." But before I could march into the eating place, Santy brought me an oatly bar. "Ta."

"Go swiftly, the moon is eager to shine."

"Come, come, we must get to the practice place." Dreng heavy-footed it to the exit. I followed whilst Orva walked behind.

When I reached the door, I paused. "Is it safe?"

"As can be. Ah, worry not. Folk will nay bother us for fear of another sound grenade being launched," Dreng said and opened the door.

Cautious as a birdybird flying too low, I stepped outside. With the S.A.N.T.S. either side of me, we tramped down the landing. Santy's voice echoing our footfalls as we descended the stairs. "Be careful. Do not Loiter. Be home before Curfew."

We went out into the almost twilight. I followed as they trekked all swiftly to the rough terrain outside Cityplace. Dreng halted just before a perimeter guard post.

"Ye may do yer practising here. We will gae to the guard hut and keep watch. We will nay interfere."

"Thanks."

"When the light fades we will return," he said and both S.A.N.T.S. strode off to the Borderguard hut. I stood looking out at the Wilderness, remembering my brief visit to it, and longed to smell and touch its loamy earthiness again.

"You may begin. The guard has turned off the fence alert in case a birdy lands," Orva called to me. I waved. Then I stared at the greying sky for a bit. "Now would be a good time."

"Fine, I'm just going to."

Huffin' hell and twice that profanity. Practice? Practice what? I had no idea how to call the birdybirds. All I knew was how to sing like them, and I had gleaned that info from an archaic slabgame. I had no desire to bring down the raptors or give folk the heebie-jeebies like before, but even from this long distance, I could feel the eyes of the two guards burning into my flesh.

Stepping closer to the fence, I lifted my head, breathed in and let out a high-pitched note. Nowt. I did it again in different keys and lengths, but no birdles called back, or flew down. I looked to the guard hut, but my safekeepers were deep in conversation with the Borderguard.

I tried several more times and just when I was about to stop, I heard a faint warble come from one of the trees in front of me. I swivelled round to see if the others had clocked the sound, but they were as before.

Leaning over the railing, I cupped my hands over my mouth and made the same tweet. It came back, closer than before. I repeated my song. I saw a rustling high up in the leaves of the tree opposite where I stood.

Again I made the sound. Before my eyes, a real live birdybird flew out of the branches.

I slapped my hands against my mouth and held my breath. The birdle swooped low before my face. I saw yellow and black feathers. It swooped again and I swear it was about to land, but a nearby rustle in the shrubbery caused it to zoom up and out of sight. Nad! My very first sight of a birdle, done for.

"Oy! Oy!" I cried out to whomever, or whatever made the distracting sound. The foliage rustling stopped. I stood on tiptoes, put my hands on top of the metal fence, and hoisted myself up so that my shoulders and head were free of its constraints. Juddering somewhat in the pecs, I shouted out again. The grass and brambles moved.

"Hey! Hey!" I near shrieked as I caught a glimpse of a shadowy form scuttling away. My muscles gave out. I fell to the ground.

"Right. The moon is rising. Best get ye back."

Coughing, I stood, brushed some muck from my kecks and nodded. Dreng looked towards the Wilderness. "What did ye see?"

I shrugged. "Nowt, really. Just saw the leaves and twigs twitch a bit. Thought it was something, wasn't I guess."

He lifted his chin and sniffed. "There's smoke upon the wind."

"So there is. Yeuk. It has a pong to it I do not care for."

Orva joined us and narrowed her already narrow eyes. "Move back, the fence is switched on. What you sniff at is Carnie stench. They roast their prey over open fires. So I heard. The smell is that of melting muscle and fat."

"Again, yeuk."

"If they are this close, we must prepare."

"For what, Dreng?"

He stared at me for too long, then spat something green onto the ground.

"Come. Adara. We must get ye to safety."

His words made my spine itch. "Hang on a sec. Are you saying that the Carnieval is here?"

"No, Dreng, is not. He is surmising that the stink we can smell, is from meat-eaters nearby." She gave her fellow Backpacker a most furrowed brow look. "This does not mean the Carnies and their mean trickery are upon us. See, the moon is almost up. Come, let us go back to your quarters."

Nothing would have suited me more, but I had a niggle-naggle nibbling on my top most vertebra. "If they are coming, then we are in trouble."

"Best not surmise that which we cannot glean."

I had no argument to Orva's sensible words, so I just shrugged and followed the S.A.N.T.S. back to Puritytowers.

## Chapter Fourteen
*Intruders*

As we strode forth, I became aware of a strange calm as if all had fallen asleep. Despite there being quite a few folk plid-plodding around trying to get as much light time as they could before Curfew Bell forced them to retreat indoors. The dark had a way of making folk jittery, especially since the Praisebee incident. What was oddly was their lack of chat. They walked all quiet-like, without purpose. I looked to Orva and Dreng; they had tightened jaws and gave out a vibe of alert.

A mist rose from the ground. It spread out in a hazy blanket that almost obscured the Citydwellers. They stopped, so did we. I peered into the mist and saw the shapes of five non-Cityfolk. How the huff did they get in? A murmur grew from where they stood. A name, mine. Huff! Not again.

The residents that stood still did not seem to notice the newcomers and joined in with the stranger's chant as if they were compelled to do so. The sound grew until 'Adara' was near shrieked.

Orva looked to Dreng. He screwed up his

eyes and scratched at his ears as though something had crawled in. The fog began to dissipate and with it the name calling. I saw the eerie cloud move swiftly towards where the oddly figures stood. It whooshed towards them as though they tugged at it. The voices that called my name grew fainter as it dispersed until it became as nowt.

In the clear that ensued five males stood wearing dark metal helmets, with blacked-out visors, so that we could not see their faces. They were dressed in all-in-one green troo suits, with a big wide belt around the middle that housed a whole host of small knives and guns. In their hands, they carried large weapons. Still folk did not seem to comprehend their sudden appearance. I was about to yell, "Oy, strange, scary looking males have mysteriously arrived," when they began to walk forward.

"Hey, ye, ye there, halt!" Dreng said.

They did not.

"Halt!"

When they did not, Orva and Dreng took out their thwacking sticks and held them out to menace the strangers.

"How the huffin' hell did they get in?"

"This is not good. You must run home. Now!" Orva said, but before I could, the hostile males hoisted their great weapons to shoulder height. She shouted out, "Stand down or we will be forced to disarm you."

They halted, dropped their weapons and cocked their heads to one side. A Citydweller fem pointed at me. "She is the Auger. Tell your Agro bosses. You can have her if you want." Then she slapped her hand over her mouth and scuttled away. The other folk stared around not knowing what to do. The helmeted ones stood stiff like statues and I wondered if they were made of flesh at all.

I turned to Orva, who was wide of eye.

"Are these Agros?"

"Must be. Or more likely, folk they have turned to do their bidding. It is said that Agros never leave their home and send others to do their filthy work. I confess to be more than puzzled by their appearance."

Dreng shrugged his ample shoulders. "They do nay seem to ha purpose. Why stand there and do nowt when they possess such mean firearms. This is strange beyond strange."

The weird Agros, if that is what they were, shuffled their feet in a dance-like manner then lifted their gun things again. "Enough of this," Ova said. She produced a head protector from her arm pouch, Dreng did the same and they put them on. The soft hat things became solid when they hit flesh, fitting snugly onto their skull and forehead. When thusly shielded, they reached into their troo leg pockets, withdrew some kind of many-bladed knife, and ran full pelt towards the enemy. To my surprise all but one of the attackers turned and fled, just like that.

A swift silence descended.

The remaining Agro stood tall and said in a low gruff voice that I could almost feel, "More are coming. We now know who and where the Auger is, thanks to your free chatting friends."

A cold wind stirred up and began to blow around the place. It became fierce. Gusty. So much so that all who remained in a trance-like state, were pushed backwards by the force of it. As it whooshed and swished, I swear I heard voices carried within it. Calling out individuals names, saying things like, "Morian, sea-born, waits for you. Cadwgan, the battle will rid you of your nearest ones. Adara, Deogol is not what he seems." I held my breath and saw the Cityfolk cower. The wind eased.

"Dreng, race to Centralplaza. Raise the

alarm."

He legged it all swiftly to said place. Pushing past the folk that clung to each other, but did not move. In but a few secs the Curfew Bell sounded. With it came several other City S.A.N.T.S. who began to mingle with the a-feared residents, pointing in the direction of the Auditorium.

Normally the Curfew Bell would send folk legging it back to their homes, this time instead of the noise forcing them to flee, it brought them forth. As well as those already outside, I saw many other Citydwellers walking about in a confused manner. The S.A.N.T.S. could not budge them. Orva shook her head, ran towards said loons, and poked and pushed them, yelling, "Fools! What is wrong with you? Curfew Bell has sounded. To your homes, quickly!"

They bumped into each other, addled and shaken. Nowt Orva or the other City S.A.N.T.S. could say made them move. They wandered about the place not knowing what to do. Then a great light came on blinding us all. The lone Agro shouted, "Stay where you are. Do not try to stop us." The light went out. The solo Agro lifted his weapon. The docile Cityfolk who knew nowt of fear or combat, stood or squatted, and let loose a most pitiful moan.

Orva stared at the intruder. "This is madness. Drop your weapon. You are alone here. We outrank you."

"That we do," Dreng said returning, and stood spread-legged, combat style. The other S.A.N.T.S. adopted the same stance.

"What do the Agros want?"

"I do nay know for certain. But they seem to be adept at creating terror amongst folk." Dreng wiped his mouth. The Agro pointed his gun at a mam carrying a bub. "What? Nay, they want to fire on kiddles too?"

"No, this is unacceptable," Orva said and raced towards the shaking Agro.

"Watch out!" I shouted as the Agro thug attempted to shoot her. Dreng lunged upon her attacker allowing her to kick him in the nads, but not before he fired a round of something nasty into Dreng. He staggered backwards then stood tall. Orva ass-kicked the Agro scum. With a grunt, he limped away.

The terrified folk gradually began to retreat from the scene of almost carnage. I ran to Orva and flung my arms around her, she hugged me close, then very swiftly pushed me away when Dreng slumped-footed over to us. "The day is won," he said then crumpled to the ground. She knelt by his side and felt his neck for a pulse.

"He lives, we must get to your home."

"Not to a medi centre? We could call for a 'ulance."

"It would take too much time." She turned to her fellow guards. "Do what you can to right things. I must take Dreng to a safe place. Adara, help me lift him."

I took an arm, Orva another, and together we hoisted Dreng to a standing position. He grunted, opened his eyes and said, "I can manage, wi yer help."

We supported his great bulk as he shuffled and wheezed all the way to the entrance to Puritytowers. When the doors whooshed open and the sanity spray washed over us, Dreng spluttered for a sec then shook us free. "I can walk unaided."

"No, you cannot. Now is not the time for futile acts of bravery. Come, rest upon my shoulder. We will take you to Breanna's quarters."

He nodded. I ran to the elevator and punched the up button. The doors slid open and Orva hobbled in with Dreng, who all but hung onto her shoulders. I stood next to him, offered my arm, he took it and up we went. It was goodly indeed that our apartment was but seven strides from the lifting room, for Dreng began to waver. Orva and I had to almost carry him to the door. I banged upon it. It opened.

"Adara, good that you are safe. Ah, not so Dreng. Come inside quick. Tell of all that has occurred."

Orva pulled Dreng back from the opened door. "Run in quick to take the blast of sanitary spray. I do not want him to inhale any more unnatural substances."

I sneezed when I took the full force of the cleansing mist. Orva helped him through the door and Santy took over from holding him up. "I am needed without, I think," Orva said. Santy nodded and Orva left us.

I closed the door. Santy near dragged Dreng into the living space and let him fall onto the comfy couch. He made an "Oof," sound then lay still on his back.

"Ah, Addly, there you are, I was worried about you when all the fuss began." I looked to the foodprep room. Greatgrangran stood in the doorway. "I heard a lot of shouting and wailing, but my game was more interesting so I went back to it. Didn't hear a thing after that," Greatgrangran said holding up a set of earhole enhancers. "Can't hear nowt but the silly tunes and effects on my slab when I wear these things." She walked in, took a swiftly look at Dreng and folded her arms. "Thought so. More fisticuffs. Such nonsense. What has occurred?"

There was a niggly feel in my nonce and an image of my bro entered my head, along with the wind words I'd heard in the plaza. "Grangran, where is Deogol?"

"Him? Sly little earwig. He is in his room, fingers near stuck to his comp pad. Oh, I asked what was what, but he scuttled past me all red of face and locked his door."

"Up to who knows what."

"Addy, why do you say that about your bro?"

I did not mean to blurt out my thoughts. Deogol was acting weirdo, though, but I wasn't going to say anything that might get him into trouble with Santy, so I changed the subject instead. "Should we not attend to Dreng's wounds?"

"I don't like blood," Greatgrangran said. "Let me know when he's bandaged up. I'm going back to my game." She turned and ambled back to Santy's resting room.

"You're right, we need to deal with Dreng. Go fetch the medikit from the cleansing area."

"Will do."

I went all quickly into the cleansingplace and opened the cupboard. In between reddy sponges and hairwash, were lots of Santy's old Backpacker med supplies. I took out several swabs, packets of some kind of pain relief, various small objects, scissors, pincers, a wad of softwool and went back. "Is there anything I can do?"

"Yes, help me take off his jacket so that we might see where he is injured."

Santy carefully lifted Dreng's shoulders a bit so that I could pull his sleeves. He gave out a moan, fluttered his eyelids and stared at me. "Ye are undressing me?"

"What? Well, in a manner of speaking," I said, then went redder than a ripe tomtom.

"Glad you have awoken. We need to get at your injuries. Try not to tease Addy so."

He winked at me and through many sucks of air that ended in, "Ow, ouch, by the Greenman himself!" Dreng wriggled out of his slashed and dirty jacket. A trickle of blood spread around his waist.

"You are oozing from the side I think."

He looked down and unbuttoned his shirt. This time Santy Breanna's cheeks tinged pink. I guess Dreng noticed because he too, despite his pallor, went a bright shade of red.

The comphone buzzed loudly, thus ending their embarrassment. Santy coughed and stood. "I'd better get that, might be urgent. Addy, tend to his wounds," she said and left.

Smiling all false-like, I pulled apart his now blood-soaked under tunic. "Yeuk and then some. You have a jaggedy gash for sure. I think some of those vile Agro metal bits are lodged within."

He winced when I touched the wound. "Ye have the skill to remove them?"

I scratched my noggin and was about to say, "Dunno, maybe, sort of," when Santy strode in.

"That was the mayor."

"He says what?"

"That we are to stay put until the all clear is sounded. There is no way of knowing whether or not more Agros are coming."

"If they do come, I'll defend ye and yers, do nay fear," Dreng said trying to stand. He did not get very far and slumped back down with a splatter of blood. Santy frowned.

"He has stuff lodged in the injury that must come out," I said.

"Go ahead. Get rid of it. I shall hand you the wipes."

"What? Me?"

"If you are to become a S.A.N.T. you

must learn much about how to treat ailments, dress wounds and the like. We have done work on this, have we not?"

"Yep, but that was make believe, this is not."

"All practice on the virtual puppets is of use. I'm sure you know what to do before delving into the real harm."

Dreng stiffened. "Erm, Breanna, perhaps it may be more prudent for ye to…"

"Nonsense. I have every faith in Addy. She is a good pupil and has steady hands. Are you afraid to let her try?"

He squinted then stuck out his chin. "Afraid? Nay. Go to it lassie."

"Are you sure?"

"Aye. Be quick."

I gulped and looked to Santy. "You have to start somewhere. I shall assist."

"Right, I'll do it, but if I barf you'll have to clean it up."

She grinned.

I rummaged around the stuff I had brought in, picked up a pair of tinytongs and blinked. Santy nodded and squirted some Sterispray on the laceration. Using a cleansing swab, I wiped the wound then delved in. With shaky fingers, I probed, gouged and yanked at the objects wedged in Dreng's flesh. He yelped now again, but remained as still as he could. Through half-closed eyes and retching most severely, I pulled out eight sharp objects. The blood came out fast. Santy handed me some bungs and I quelled the flow as best I could.

"All gone?"

I peered into the large slash on Dreng's waist.

"Yep."

"Be certain. For if even a tiny sliver of that Agro weaponry is left behind, then a most severe infection will ensue."

Puffing out my cheeks, I took in a deep breath, so did Dreng. With shaking fingers, I parted the wound. His muscles went into spasm. I quickly grabbed the lightfibre torch Santy held out. Swallowing hard, I searched the grizzly opening for signs of metal and the like. "All clean." Dreng relaxed. Santy gave me the softwool, bandages and tape.

"You will have to hold the pad in place so that I can secure it," I said.

Santy held the swab against Dreng's flesh with such tenderness that I almost blushed for them both. Quickly ridding my skull of the picture of Santy and Dreng in a pash, I pressed Stickystrips all round the dressing, then indicated for Dreng to sit up a little so that I could wind the bandage around his middle. When I was done, I sat back on my knees and whistled through my teeth.

"Ye will make a good S.A.N.T. Adara, ye are brave and resourceful."

"Thanks to Santy Breanna."

Dreng sat upright. "Shame my tunic is of no use."

Santy narrowed her eyes. "Here, hand it over. I'll wash and dry it for you in a few secs."

He lifted one side of his mouth and said all flirty-like, "Will ye help me undress then?"

With a raised eyebrow, Santy slowly peeled away his sodden under shirt.

Yeuk! Both were nearing oldie age and acting like juves. In front of me. I thought best to turn them from their lustful carryings on. "Right, well, I'll take that. Slam it in the washpod, okay?" I said and grabbed the garment. As I sped into the foodprep room where said appliance was, I asked, "So, did the mayor have any suggestions as to why the Agros have come now?"

"No one knows for sure. Some think it is to do with you and your gift, whilst others believe it maybe something concerning the Praisebees."

"I was named in front of them."

"Ah, do not worry, there is more to this than your whereabouts I think."

I threw Dreng's tunic into the whirlywash. As the thing spun round and round, my thoughts went back to the time I spent with Elijah and Lilith. I remembered some of the things she told me. I went back into the room where Santy and Dreng sat all cosy-like. "The Priasebee notion could be right Santy, for when I was locked away with them, the fem divulged that they had been plotting an attack on Cityplace for some time. Yet the way they live would suggest to me that they would not have the means to procure the bombs they used upon us."

"But, Agros do have such nasty weaponry. Adara, ye have been of use again," Dreng said and for some reason that made me smile.

"Now, it is time for the injured to rest. Addy, go rouse your bro. Tell him to quit whatever he is doing and come here for some chat. Dreng will take his quarters and sleep until the time for action is upon us."

## Chapter Fifteen
*Waiting For The All Clear*

I plodded heavy-headed to Deogol's room and tapped on the door. There was nowt in way of response. I tapped again and called his name.

"Go away."

"Santy wants you out so that Dreng can lie down and recover from his injuries."

"He is badly hurt?"

"Not so much, but would benefit from a slumber so his bod can heal a bit."

I heard a rapid tip-tapping then the firm closing of a comp lid. A few secs went by then the door opened. My bro stood staring at me with bloodshot eyes. I pointed at his peepholes and he rubbed them. "Too much screen watching. Santy said it would do you harm."

"Yep, I know, I know. Greatgrangran went on about the same thing too. Then sat down and stuck her mush into the slab game. Double standards or what?"

I gave over to feelings of suspish. Deogol was never one to reason so philosophically before. Normally he wouldn't care two howlet hoots what any of us did. "Well," I said, "she is an oldie after all."

"So, she should set an example for me to follow, not the other way round." He clenched his hands on saying the words and I became uneasy with his black mood.

"Calmly Bro."

"I am calm. Shall we go?" he said and pushed past me, clutching onto his lapcomp.

When we arrived in the kinsfolk room, Santy and Dreng were guffawing loudly. On hearing us enter, they changed their mood to serious.

"Ah, good you have relinquished your sleeping quarters for Dreng to use."

Deogol pouted and shrugged.

"Do you need assistance to get there?"

"Nay Adara, but many ta's for asking." With a great effort, Dreng lifted himself from the cosycouch and walked all-hunched up like to my bro's resting place.

"Hungry?"

"Strangely, no."

"Mmmm. Strange indeed, Adara. Deogol, would you care for some grub?"

"Not now Santy." He plonked his behind down on the chair opposite her., opened his comp and tapped upon the keypad. I gave Santy a raised eyebrow look. She shook her head.

"What preoccupies you so, little Earwig?"

With a huge sigh, Deogol lifted his gaze from the flickering screen. "Please refrain from calling me that bub's name."

"My apologies. What is it that compels you so to stare into that comp with such intensity?"

"You would not understand. It is beyond your brawny ways."

"Oy, Bro, less lip."

He snorted. "It is the truth."

"Not the point. Show respect to the one that helped you grow."

"I am surrounded by thickies," he said and returned to whatever he was watching.

Santy stood. For a moment, I thought she was going to admonish him, but she did not. Instead, she beckoned for me to follow. I did. We went out into the landing are. "Things are looking bleak. The mayor is unable to contact the Agros to discover why they sent in their troops. Folk are scared and there is no info to help quell fears, if they can be quelled."

"Another onslaught is inevitable though?" A sigh was the answer to my question. "I do not like being so in the dark. Mebbe there is news without?" I said and made my way to the staircase.

"Do not venture outside. We do not know what awaits."

Sucking in oxy, I raced down the steps. When I arrived at the exit, Santy was already there. "Huffin' hell, how do you do that?"

"Run past when you are least expecting it. That is all. A trick of the mind when it is elsewhere occupied. The skill is in knowing the moment, and that comes with practise."

I peered over her shoulder to see if there was any movement from friend or foe, but it was moontime. I saw nowt. "I am itchy to know more. It is too quiet. What if we went together?"

"My thoughts exactly. I too cannot stand to wait for an onslaught, much rather have an inkling when it will begin. Let us be quick."

I nodded.

Santy pressed the open button. A blast of cold air met us as we raced out of the building, not stopping until we reached Centralplaza. I expected it to be full of citizens, but it was not. We slowed and stopped outside the auditorium, where but a few moons ago I was collecting my sham award for finishing classes I paid no heed to.

It was so still and quiet that I could almost

believe that nowt had occurred in the way of turmoil. Normally there was some kind of noise, even if it was just the infoboard giving out the news of the day in a nasal compvoice.

The only evidence of battle was the bits of torn off clothing, ammo and blood that littered the floor. If it weren't for the threat of Agro, a purifying team would have swept it clean in a sec or two. I looked to the vidscreen in the centre of the square. For the first time that I was aware of, it was blank.

"This calmness is most unnatural," Santy said and strode around the square, cocking her head to listen for any kind of sound. She was not to be disappointed, for all of a sudden-like, there came a huge boom as though the sky had cracked and all the objects that lay beyond it had fallen through the gap, landing with a burst.

I squatted. Santy raced to where I crouched. Bits of debris fell fast. We had to roll and dodge so as to escape the stone and rubble that near hit us. Smoke billowed around the square then another bang blast sent us staggering backwards. The end of Curfew bell sounded.

"What the huff? Santy," I shouted, "what gives? Why ring the bell to bring folk forth when clearly they should not?"

Santy grabbed my arm. "I have no clue, but can guess that this is yet another Agro raid upon us. I further guess it is they who rang the bell to lure folk out."

Sneaky. Still it worked, for I spied through the diminishing mist, Cityfolk and to my amazement, Praisebees, scurrying this way and that.

I was about to ask Santy what they were running from, when I saw some Agro army males that had so suddenly appeared then disappeared, rounding up the Praisebees. After shoving them forward towards the city exit, they turned upon the crowd. Santy took my hand. We ran and hid behind the infoboard as the Agro thugs raised their weapons.

"Down!" came a cry. From the direction of the Decontamination House came the familiar shape of Orva accompanied by some of her City S.A.N.T. guards. Santy showed herself to them. Orva called over, "They have stormed the Decontamination House. Freed the Praisebees. Hide yourself quick." Her words were lost as the Agro force opened fire. They shot round after round of those horrible nail things and many of our folk fell injured. I saw the Praisebees cower behind their guards and put their arms over their heads.

Nad.

Something nasty was about to occur. An Agro thug pushed his way through the turmoil and let loose a projectile. It landed on the ground smack in the middle of where everyone lay.

It quivered.

We held our breath.

Nowt came out, just a loud bang.

Orva and the other S.A.N.T.S. came to a halt. "Move! Now!"

All stood.

The Agros and Praisebees ran quicker than quick. Cityfolk backed away from the object that stuck out from the ground like a simple pole. I turned my head in the direction of where the Praisebees and Agro army had fled, but saw nowt.

The bomb exploded.

Bods flew into the air, landing hard on the ground. Dust swirled, smoke plumed, yells and screams near deafened me. Before Santy or I could do anything but cough, there came another great bang. The whole place seemed to shudder. I lost my footing and Santy had to grab my arm to stop me from falling. Through the haze of chaos, I saw street lamps fall and folk stagger around all befuddled.

"Get cover! Go! Now! To the Auditorium. Quick!" Orva ran amongst the injured and confused, shouting instructions. The other S.A.N.T.S. did their best to steer folk up the steps. We emerged from our hiding place and went with fleet-foot to the same place.

Two fems, dressed in bedtime clothes pushed past us and ran shrieking for the steps as another great bang sent chunks of buildings crashing down around us.

Folk lay strewn around the square. Some were moaning, trying to stand, others lay motionless. I could not help but gulp when I saw a bub crawl from underneath a blood-soaked bod. I raced to the tot, bundled it up in my arms and felt a hand on my shoulder.

"Addy. Give the kiddle to me, you are injured."

A sharp pain in my forearm almost made me drop the bubby. I handed it over to Santy She took the newbie from my grasp and pushed me towards the Auditorium. I held my hand over the wound to stop the blood that gushed from it and continued up the stairs. At the top, I saw many Cityfolk piling in. We were near squashed in the rush to get through and out of harms way. Eventually, we were able to enter. I gasped when I saw the horror inside. It looked more like a Trauma Room than a rec venue. Medics tended to the sick and injured on makeshift beds, which were no more than blankies on the floor.

Santy handed the bub to a nursey, then took me to the back of the stage. "How is your injury?"

I lifted my hand and saw no free flowing blood. "Nowt but a scratch."

"Things are bad Addy. We must return to Deogol and Greatgrangran."

I did not need to be told twice.

Giving Orva a friendly wave as we left the relative safety of the building, we headed for the exit. Stepping over rubble, Santy and I raced through the carnage, back to Puritytowers.

## Chapter Sixteen
*Calm Before The Storm*

Once away from the main plaza, the noise and smell of combustibles eased. I did not notice the gash on my left arm until we reached the entrance of our Homeblock. It began to throb. When I looked down, I saw that it was deep, dirty, and had something stuck in it.

Santy opened the doors. We ran into the hallway. All was calm. Clean as normal. However, our muckiness attracted the dirt sensors. I heard a click and buzz sound as the disinfectant spray nozzles in the ceiling came on. A pitiful amount of cleansing fluid came out and merely dribbled onto the floor.

"So it begins."

"So what begins?"

"Things going wrong."

"Ow."

"Your wound is angry, Addy."

"Seems so." I held my arm up so that she could take a peek.

"Nasty. It needs cleaning out and joining together. Come, there's enough Medstuff at home for that."

We made our way up the stairs slowly,

both suffering the effects of our fast pace to reach Puritytowers. My legs ached and my wound hurt badly. I wanted more than anything to be in my own restroom. Santy's breathing was forced. Another thing I had not noticed in the confusion of escape. Also, her face was bruised on one side, her eye black and swollen.

"That must hurt."

"What?"

"You have sustained a bruise above your left eye."

She touched it and flinched. "That I have."

We soon came to our abode. Santy went to swish the door with the cardkey thingy, but it was flung open by Dreng, who stood holding his hand over his face. He removed it revealing a great puffiness and swelling on his right cheek.

"Dreng what happened to you?

"Deogol."

"What, my weakling bro did this?"

"Aye."

He stepped aside and we walked into the kinsroom."

"When the Agros began their assault, he became agitated. Demanded to gae into the fray. He gave me quite a thwack when I blocked his escape."

The fact that my bro had attacked a S.A.N.T. and caused him harm, was upsetting, but, I was impressed. I never thought him capable of inflicting such a powerful blow. Santy must have read my thoughts, or just noticed the one-sided grin on my face. "I am in awe of his clout ability. Apologies Dreng, he should not have thwacked you."

"He should not. I overpowered him. Ye need not fear, I have not harmed the laddie, merely given him a calmative, just in case he tried to manhandle Amranwen. He should still be sleeping."

Greatgrangran entered holding a large pot.

"Where is Deogol?"

"In his room Grangran. Asleep."

"Good. I locked myself in when I heard him become restless. He called out some names I did not recognise, so I took the precaution of arming myself."

Santy took the object from her shaking hand and led her to the cosycoach. "Sit down, I'll go check on Deogol. Then see about fixing you up Addy."

"What's wrong Adellia? Did you get caught up in that hullabaloo?"

"Yep." I showed her my injury.

"Oh, that's nowt but a scratch." She smiled and patted the cushion next to her. "Come, sit next to me." I did. She smoothed back some damp hair from my forehead. "You have pluck in abundance."

"Ta, Grangran."

Santy returned with a whole tray full of Medistuff and sat beside me.

"Deogol still sleeps, so I thought it best to leave him. Come, Addy, let me tend to your wound. Yours too Dreng."

He shook his head. "Nay need. I'll spray some coolant on. Let nature do the rest."

Santy handed him said healing jet and he gave his cheek a goodly coating. "Right, that arm needs tending, Adara. I see some debris in there so will have to yank it out. I swear I saw Dreng smirk. Santy took an anaesthetic jet bottle and gave my arm a spray. "Has it gone numb?"

I nodded, sat stiff and winced more than once when she dug around with the tweezers to extract the blobs of muck lodged in the wound. She squirted some antibacterial solution all around, squeezed the cut together, stapled it shut, then sprayed some Synthskin on top.

"I don't think you'll be left with a scar."

"Nice work Santy, ta."

"You have a look of weariness about you Addy, you should go and rest."

I shook my head. Too much was occurring for me to contemplate a snooze. "Nah, I'm too hyped. Besides, I wish to know more of Deogol and his new-found fisticuff skills."

"Nay much to tell. He went a little wild, gave me a thwack when I least expected it. That is that," Dreng said and went slightly pink.

Greatgrangran whistled through her teeth. "Oh, I'll tell what I know. That young 'un has changed. I blame all that corrupt info he looks at on that slab of his. I told you not to give it to him."

"Gran, all the kiddles have them."

"Nay, not all, just the privileged few, and the Meeks."

There was a look of displeasure on Dreng's face as he said those words. I wondered if he resented all that Cityfolk kiddles had, knowing how his own kin went without any form of tech. Being that they lived inside trees and all.

"He has been spending too much time on the thing, behaving furtively when drawn to the point." We all nodded at Santy's words.

"I had a gander at a site he wa on when I slipped him a stupifier. Agro speak. All of it.

Telling of a better world for those not called norms. Telling of how the 'Lost Ones' as they put it, would be that nay longer. And worse, telling of a place that has all the latest tech and the like. What Meek would nay be tempted by such promises?"

Santy stood and folded her arms. "Fake promises. Agro lies. They are planning something nasty make no mistake. It is common knowledge that Meeks have been disappearing in other places. That food is being withheld and skirmishes breaking out all over NotSoGreatBritAlbion."

Greatgrangran shook her head and picked up her bitsandbobsbag that lay on top of the small, round glass table. "The world as we know it is changing. Glad I won't be around to have to live through it. I like my humble existence the way it is. I was going to ask Deogol to fix my portaplay. Perhaps when he is feeling more himself you can give it to him. At my time of life, I have little pleasures left," she said, pulled out an redundant early version of her slab and handed it to Santy.

"He will make it right. He fixed the screen on the comdevice in a few secs, so this will not tax him too greatly. Besides, he is in trouble. Making your pastime work again will be a worthy punishment."

"Goodly good. I would like to go back to Goldenagehome now. I feel safer around the oldies. No Agro would bother to injure a bunch of ancients about to mingle with the wormies," she said and eased herself out of the comfy cushions.

Santy put the device down. "We do not know if all is safe."

"I want to go." Greatgrangran slapped her bag down hard against the table. "Now, do you hear me?"

Wincing, Santy looked to Dreng. He shrugged. "We could try. I think the booms and bangs have stopped for the moment."

"For the moment. Right. We will have to go around the far side of the plaza. Too much debris for you to flounder on otherwise. I will be back as soon as Addy." She leant close and whispered, "Keep a close watch on Deogol. If he wakes before my return, divert his mind from escape with Greatgrangran's playthingy."

"Will do. Return safe and sound."

"Are we to go now?" Greatgrangran said, tapping her foot.

"Indeed, let us." Santy held out her hand, Grangran took it and they started for the exit.

"I shall accompany ye. Do nay fear, my injuries are greatly healed. I can be of use."

"Your presence will be appreciated," Santy said. Out of the room, they went again all blushing and the like.

"Mush," Grangran said. Then she turned to me. "Bye Addree."

"Bysiebye Greatgrangran."

"Oh, I have no brain left, that's for sure. Here Adra, I meant for you to have this on your leaving day." She bent down and pulled at something from behind the comfychair. "There. Hope you like it."

"Like it? A Synthbag! Ta." I flew off the cosycouch and took the high-tech thing from her outstretched hands.

"Put it on, see how it feels."

I threw the bag onto my back and slid on the shoulder straps.

"Careful of your arm," Santy said as she came back in. But I had forgot all about it in the rush to try out the sac. I turned around to show them both. "What a wondrous thing it is. Utterly invisible Addy. Can you feel it?"

I wriggled my shoulders until the bag rested comfortably between them. "Nope. It's as if it was not there at all."

"Thought you'd like it."

I gave my grangran a hug and she grunted.

"My how strong you have become. Enjoy your prezzie."

"Let your grangran go, Addy, I wish to have her back and return before anything else occurs. There is no knowing what the Agros have planned next. Plus, the explosions have affected our tech. Lights and security cams could be down, or worse, all of the perimeter fence."

Releasing Greatgrangran, I walked her to the door and waved as she left. Although I was well impressed with my gift, a dread still lingered in my bowels. I hoped for the safe return of my Santy. I took off the Synthbag and looked inside. There were pockets, hidden places, and I spent many secs peeking, discovering compartment after compartment. At the bottom was a small sealed pouch. I pulled it open then gasped at what I saw. Sterichoc. Six bars of it. This stuff was worth all the seeds in Cityplace. Well maybe not all, just a handful. Greatgrangran was full of surprises. I resisted the urge to gobble them down and sealed the secret chamber back up. In light of recent troubles, I could not be sure when and where such stuffs would be able to be procured.

I fondled the material. It was soft and

smooth to the touch. This bag was truly special. It was as light as a bub's eyelash, as strong as nanorope, and as see-through as a raindrop when it came into contact with its owners heartbeat. The Synthbag was a thing all the girlygigs in Cityplace hankered after. The only other fem I knew that had one was Drysi. She only used it to keep her facepaint in. Now that I owned one I could fill it with goodies and things to help in a scrap.

What with all the trouble brewing I intended to keep the thing on me at all times. I grabbed some of the Medistuff that Santy used to heal my wound and went into the cleansingroom.

I packed in more essential survival things, such as reddysponges, I was due any sec, plus, a whole host of cleaning things. Next I ventured into the foodpreproom and opened the grub cupboard.

Huff, hardly any food. I couldn't bring myself to snatch the few remaining cartons of soylygrub, so rooted around at the back until I came across packages stuffed there because no one wanted to eat them. I took out two packs of instant pea-like soup then to my glee discovered a crumpled sachet of soymadras and soysausage. They went in too.

I skipped into my layingdownroom. Once there, I took out various bits of clothing and packed them in as well. I marvelled at how much I could fit into such a small thing. When I thought it was filled to capacity with necessaries, I put it on. It still felt as light as before. I was baffled, also in awe of such tech. I wondered if Deogol would be able to tell me how it worked. My gut twisted round. Nad. The reddies. I sloped off into the cleansingarea, and packed my bloody bits with a reddysponge.

On the way back to my resting place, I thought I heard murmuring from my bro's room. I stood outside his door and pressed my ear to it. All I could hear was a faint nasal snuffling. I opened it and went inside. Deogol looked so peaceful, so innocent. I could not believe his recent bad behaviour, and could not recall him ever lashing out. Not even at a fly when we picnicked in Citypark for his tenth comingoutday.

I went to his side and put my hand on his shoulder to wake him. His eyes snapped open. He stared wildly for a sec then focused on me.

He raised his head and said, "I need to go."

## Chapter Seventeen
*The Storm Approaches*

"Deogol, stay. You are not allowed to leave." He pushed me to one side and jumped out of bed. I grabbed him around the waist causing him to fall back. He struggled to free himself, but I managed to flip him over and pin down his arms. He kicked. Fought like a Wolfie in a trap. It was all I could do to keep him from breaking free. My arm hurt and I did not want to ruin the repair work that Santy had done on it, so I let go his arms and sat on his stomach.

"Ow. Ow. Get off me you pudgy wastesac."

"No, not until you swear that you won't try to run."

Deogol squirmed then dug his fingers into my back. I pulled his hands away and held onto his wrists. "I am stronger than you. You will never beat me." He wriggled like a wormie in the sun. Truth be told, I was having difficulty keeping him down.

"Let me go."

"Not until you swear that you will stay put." I pressed my ample butt down upon his belly. He made a breathy yell then lay still.

"You're killing me with your bulk."

"I am not. Now, promise to keep still or I will sit lower down and squish your nads."

Deogol made a sound not unlike being sick, then I felt his bod go limp.

"I promise, now get off."

I did and stood by the door in case he meant to make a run for it. He didn't, instead he got up and went to his comp. Back to the Deogol I knew. He sat tiptapping as if I wasn't there. I coughed, he looked up. "What?"

"Are you communing with Agros?" He did not answer and continued to type. "Deogol, answer me."

"Go away, I'm busy."

Realising I would get nowt but antsy from my bro, I thought it would be a goodly plan to divert his somewhat dubious attention from the ether of the airwaves, to something more tangible. I ran all quick-like into the kinsfolk room and picked up the broken portaplay.

When I returned to my bro he was leaning forward, staring hard at something on the screen. I tiptoed up behind him and saw a picture of a room filled with plants, cosycouches, foodstuffs of every kind. Techcomps the like I had never seen. I involuntarily said, "Wow, that is some plush place and no mistake."

Deogol slammed down the lid and turned to me.

"Are you spying on me now?"

"Me? Nah, just wondering what it is you're gawping at?"

"Nowt, just a game."

"Yeah? Goodly graphics, very realistic."

"That is what they are like now. You wouldn't know because you do not use comps."

"Don't need to access said device."

"Because you can't."

"Can, don't want to."

"Oh yeah? How do you access the infosite on here?" he said and folded his arms.

"I don't have to show you, you already know. Enough of your backchat, Greatgrangran wants you to fix her playslab." I held it out, he snorted.

"Does it have to be now?"

"Yes. Do you not know what the huff has been happening outside?"

"Of course I do. More than you."

"What does that mean?" He did not answer me and turned back to his comp. "Explain."

"Nowt to explain," he said then looked at

me over his shoulder. "Give me the thing." I handed it to him. "You don't have to be here while I fix it."

"Yep, I do. Santy told me to watch. I will do just that."

He shrugged turned to his desk and began to fiddle with the toy. I watched him press buttons, tap info with such speed and assurance that he lost his look of kiddle, and took on the appearance of 'dult. Despite my interest in his working, I became drowsy. My head lolled. I felt compelled to lie down on his bed. Deogol continued to twiddle and type. I drifted off to slumberland.

There was a low rumble outside. At first I thought it explosives in the distance, but a flash of light through the window suggested that it was thunder. I rubbed my eyes and sat up. Deogol was gone. I raced into every room, but he was not there. Santy would be more than angry with me. I went to his comp, pressed a button and the screen came on. I tapped my finger on a symbol that looked like a mouth. A whole load of comtext appeared. I read but two before racing out of the room, down the stairs and outside.

The sky was dark with grey clouds that rolled and grumbled as they approached. I looked up at the lightning rod. Although I feared storms and stayed in my room when they happened, finding Deogol put the fright to the back of my nonce.

I used the tracking know-how that Santy taught me and searched the soft earth for signs of footfall. There were many. I bent low to see if I could distinguish my bro-bro's uneven tread. He walked with a slight prominence to his left side, which meant that he pressed said foot harder to the ground than with the other. There amongst the comings and goings of those that dwelled in the building, I saw Deogol's trademark step.

It was fresher than the rest. I was grateful that the rain had not come down. I quickened my pace and followed his tracks to the City perimeter. They stopped by the guard hut, which to my surprise was empty. I looked inside. There was blood splattered on the walls, ceiling and floor. I guessed said guard had been injured then gone to seek assistance.

I peered over the fence. The ground was covered with signs of someone walking into the trees ahead. Broken foliage, disturbed bushes and indented earth, were a giveaway. I bent down, picked up a rock and threw it against the fence. When the alarm did not sound I climbed over and walked stealthily in the direction of the bruised undergrowth. No wonder any folk could enter. The perimeter guards all gone and the warning alert turned off. My skin hairs poinged upright.

Stepping uneasily for a few secs before hearing voices not too far in the distance, I stopped, listened, and recognised my bro talking. I tiptoed closer. Through the twigs and leaves, I saw Deogol deep in convo with a tall stranger. The unfamiliar figure wore a hooded tunic that obscured its face, but I could see enough to know that it was male.

Not many fems that I have come into contact with sported face hair. He handed my bro a small square metal box. Deogol quickly put it into his pocket. The 'dult bent down to my bro and spoke to him in a hushed voice. The male finished what he was saying, shook Deogol's hand and scurried off into the density of the trees. I stepped back, hid among the greenery and watched my bro make his way back towards Cityplace.

I waited until he was out of sight, then followed. The rain came down heavy. As I ran through the droplets, I wished I'd taken a waterproof pelt with me before leaving.

Needless to say, I was soaked when I reached Puritytowers. Shaking the excess water off, I bounded up the stairs to our place, hoping to see Santy. She had not returned, so I went straight into Deogol's room. He was sitting at his comp as if nothing had occurred. I stood in the doorway, my arms folded. Without looking up, he said, "I've fixed Greatgrangran's toy."

"What were you doing in the Wilderness? Who were you speaking too?What was it he gave you?" I thought my bro would bluster and redden at my words, but he did not waver from his tappings and replied as though the matter was unimportant.

"Nowt. I was just went for a stroll, when this 'dult turned up. Nowt was planned or the like. I was curious, that is all."

"Lies Deogol. Now give me the truth before Santy Breanna comes back."

"You wouldn't understand."

"Probably not, but give forth the info I asked for anyway."

"Things are changing. I want to be part of that."

"Explain"

Deogol turned his head and stared at me with such a look of solemnity that my insides turned up and over with deep concern. "I cannot as yet. I don't have all the info, but I have learned that there is a place that is apt for those like me."

"Yes. That place is here, not anywhere else."

He turned back to his comp, "I knew you would say that."

"Deogol?"

"I have no more to say."

"I will have to tell Santy that you went out for a clandestine rendezvous with quite possibly an Agro."

My bro's shoulders stiffened. He stood, faced me and clenched his fists. I saw a fierce look in his eyes. "Do not tell. You must not say what you saw. It is nothing, I told you. I was sick from being inside and needed the openness to freshen my brain."

"You do not enjoy the outdoors Deogol, tell the truth."

"That is it. You know there are many strangers out and about now. Why would you not believe that I could have met up with one without prior arrangement?"

"You never go out. Suspish that you do, then meet up with a stranger, especially in these dangerous times?"

"All folk are strangers to me, you know

that, why would this 'dult be any different."

I had no answer to that. Deogol did indeed find other folk hard to deal with; it was part of his Meekness. He sat back down. "You are dripping. Maybe you should dry yourself before Santy gets back?"

"I will, but not before you tell me what you have in your pocket."

"This?" he said and took out the thing I saw him take from the probable Agro. "This is a playslab, nothing more."

"Oh really? What games does it have?"

"Don't know, haven't tried it yet. You can use it later if you like."

"Mebbe I can use it now. Hand it over."

My bro clutched onto the thing and shook his head. "No. It was given to me, I will use it first."

He had a mean look in his eyes. His fingers began to turn white from the effort of holding on to the dubious object. "Right, fine. I'll go change my clothes," I said and left.

As I walked to my room the storm became fierce. Cracks of lightning and crashes of thunder sent shivers up and down my back. I raced to my quarters, quickly put on some dry garments and returned to Deogol's room. I pushed on the door, but it would not yield. I tried again, same result. I banged upon it. I shouted out his name, but no response came forth. I was puzzled in the extreme since there were no locks to secure said portals. I continued to bang and shout until I felt a hand on my shoulder. I swizzled round. "Santy. Where is Dreng?"

"He remains with the oldies. What is the problem?"

"Deogol has barricaded himself in."

Santy pushed me aside and gave the door a goodly shove. It budged a bit so she tried again. "Help me. I think he has placed something heavy against it. After three, kick it as hard as you are able." She counted and on, "Three," we gave it a mighty boot. It opened enough for us to lean our shoulders against the wood. We shoved until there was a gap big enough for us to slip through.

"Deogol?" Santy said and rushed over to his prone bod. Slumped over his comp, with his head pressed down on the keypad. His arm hung limply by his side. On the floor at his feet, was the box the stranger had given him. Santy pulled him to a sitting position, knelt down, put her fingers on his neck and cocked her ear to his mouth. "Alive. Take his legs, we can lift him to the bed."

He was easy to carry, being long and slim

built. I gulped down the fear that was swelling in my throat and laid his legs gently on the mattress. Santy sat on the edge and held onto his hand. I picked up the box and brought it over for her to inspect. "What is this?"

"A stranger gave it to him."

"What? When did a stranger call?"

I looked to the floor. If I told the truth then not only would my bro be in big trouble, but I too. "Erm."

"Adara, I will know if you are lying."

"Deogol went out."

Santy took in a sharp breath of air. "Where you with him?"

"Yes and no."

"Adara, this is serious."

"I fell asleep. When I woke, he was gone. So I went outside and tracked him to the edge of the Wilderness. He was speaking with a 'dult. Not Cityfolk. Maybe Agro."

"Agro? Is that where he got this box?"

I nodded. Santy opened it. She looked inside, put her hand on her forehead and said, "Poisonpills."

## Chapter Eighteen
*Blackout*

"Should we call firstaiders?"

"No time. Get the Medicase."

I ran to Santy's restingroom and pulled out a red box from underneath her bed. It was her special Backpacker kit containing fixing things not normally found in regular med cupboards. I went to where Deogol lay and handed it to her. She opened it, withdrew a small phial, snapped off the top, lifted my bro's head and let the liquid drop onto his lips. I watched it slowly seep into his mouth. Within a few secs, he sat up.

"Fetch a large pot from the foodpreproom. Quickly."

I did. Santy grabbed it and Deogol barfed up what looked like his entire life's worth of grub. The pot soon filled. I gagged when Santy told me to empty it and bring it back. My bro filled the thing three more times, before falling back onto the bed. His face was whiter than the sheets he lay upon and his whole bod shook. Santy took a Freshwipe and gently mopped his face.

"Is he better?

"I think so. We don't know when he took

the tablets, so there might be some residual poison left."

There was a sweet, acrid smell of vom throughout the room. I retched and went to the cleansingroom for something freshly scented to block out the odour. The lights did not go on when I entered the place. I had to bang the console before they did. Even then they merely flickered and gave off such dimness that I could barely see enough to procure the perfume spray. But spy it I did and took it. Then I returned to Deogol's room.

He was snoozing. I filled the air with the odour-masking fragrance. Santy Breanna was leaning forward, elbows on her knees, hands clenched as if she were a Praisebee in prayer mode. I touched her shoulder. She flinched and turned to face me. "Tell me everything about this meeting with a stranger."

"I told all."

"Did you hear any conversation?"

"Nope. I was too far away."

"Did Deogol seem upset?"

"No more than usual when he is interrupted from his musings on that thing." I pointed to his comp, went over to it and switched it on. "He was looking at some pictures he said was a game, but I am not so sure. He also said something about there being a special place for those like him."

Santy stood beside me. I touched an icon at the top of the screen. The image I'd seen before appeared. Santy bent close. "This is Agro stuff. Propaganda. I have seen similar picks from yesteryear. Not long after the Greatplague of 2086. The Agros began their dominance over the land. Tried to force folk into work camps and the like. That's partly the reason why the country is split the way it is."

"Santy, do you think Deogol was on to something when he said that the Agros want to bring folk together again?"

"Highly doubtful. Agros only want to use folk. Addy, access the infochannel."

"Erm, don't know how?"

"Are you sporting with me?"

"Nope. Not really compfriendly."

"But you used them at the Learningplace didn't you?"

"Well, yeah, suppose but they were the old style comps. Deogol's is newer and far more sophisticated."

Santy shook her head and touched several symbols that were neatly stacked at each corner of the screen. Some did nowt, others just showed numbers and odd calculations. Finally, she tapped on one and on came the infochannel. The headline read: 'Agro assault on Cityplace causes havoc. There are Reports of unrest in other sections of NotSoGreatBritAlbion. Two more cases of Meeks going missing from Woodsfolk camps.' Santy closed the lid.

"Agros are up to no good." She went to Deogol and rolled up the sleeve of his tunic. "Hand me the hypo from my kit." I did. Santy plunged it into his arm and sucked up a quantity of blood. My bro twitched a bit, then relaxed into his sleepy state once more.

Santy shuffled around in her medbag and brought out a pack of multi-coloured swabs. She squirted a drop of Deogol's blood onto each one, then placed them on the lid of the box. "We will have to wait a few secs."

"For what?"

"To see exactly what it was that the Agros gave your bro."

"Poisonpills, we know."

"I don't think they are. He is too sleepy. You see, Adara, poisonpills would not cause his comatose state. Besides, Deogol is not a selfkiller, despite what he said about the Decontamination Place. He was under no threat."

"Is it a ploy by the Agros?"

"Not sure. But it is clear that they mean to take more Meeks. For what purpose I cannot tell."

Santy picked up the swabs, took out a chart thing and held each one up to various colours on the sheet. One such hue matched perfectly. "Purple. Confirmation that he did not take a lethal substance."

"What did he take?"

"Mindfreetabs."

"Aren't they the most illegal thing in all this ever diminishing land?"

"Only Agros and Ladies have access to them."

"Why would he take them?"

"Only he knows the answer."

My bro's comp came to life by itself. The lid popped open and the screen came on. There was the same image I saw before. We backed away and turned to Deogol. Still sleeping, he raised himself from the bed, and, as if in a trance, walked to the machine. He opened his eyes, sat down and began to tap on the keyboard.

"Deogol," I said, he did not answer. "We must wake him."

"No Addy, let's see what's what."

We moved a little closer and saw that he

was typing questions asking about the place that was for Meeks only. The answers were persuasive. They spoke of stuff that only Meeks would comprehend. Things like all the tech they could imagine and more. No wonder my bro was so keen. Then some random numbers appeared and the screen went black. My bro slumped in his seat. Santy pulled me away.

"We must not let Deogol out of our sight."

I agreed.

Together we picked him up and placed him back onto the bed. Santy went to the small window opposite the compdesk and secured it. She put the key into her pocket and picked up his comp. "No more chat with Agro scum that's for sure. Addy, you take the first watch. If he comes round, call me." I nodded. She packed away all the stuff from the medicase and left me alone with my snoozing bro.

The storm raged less. I went to the window and looked out. The infoboards outside were working again. They flashed pic after pic of the Agro invaders. I was too far away to be able to read the words that scrolled underneath each image, but guessed they were similar to those Santy and I read on Deogol's comp. The lights flickered both inside and out. At first, I thought it was lightning. Wrong. The infoboard images twitched and split then became nowt more than a series of disconnected shapes before the giant screen went blank.

All the lights went out.

"Addy, stay where you are, do not leave Deogol. Do you hear me?"

"Yes."

A bright beam flashed in my face. I covered it with my hand. "Lower the torch." She did and shone it onto Deogol's bed. He was resting like a newbie after feeding, unaware of anything that was happening around him. I went to Santy. She handed me another torch.

"Quickly, go get the lightsticks from the foodpreproom. I'll stay with Deogol."

I did as she said and brought in all the neonglows that I found. I tapped two on the wall and they gave forth a cheery orange light that illuminated the room. I placed one on the comptable and the other on the windowsill. They produced enough light for us to switch off our torches. I sat on the edge of his bed. Santy sighed. "The comp's not working either."

"Agros?"

"Most likely."

"Do you think they mean to attack again?"

"I think they do."

"Well, they'll get in without much bother. There was no guard at the perimeter fence when I was there searching for Deogol. The alarm was off too."

There was a loud banging on the front door and a voice called out, "Is anyone in there?"

Santy stood and called back, "Yes."

"You must come out. You must come with us to the Auditorium. We fear another Agro assault is imminent. All power has been cut to Cityplace. We must take all Cityfolk to the same place for safety."

"We have a sickly young 'un."

"Open and I will help carry them."

Santy left to let in the Buildingprotector. I gathered up some clothes for us all, then went to my room and slipped on my Synthbag. Santy entered with Brychan, the 'dult in charge of safety for all in Puritytowers. He was a tall male with light red hair and as his name suggested, a whole host of brown speckly dots upon his skin. When Deogol and I were young, we wondered about joining them all together to see what kind of picture they would make. He nodded to me and followed us to my bro's room.

"What ails the lad? Nowt contagious?" He put his hand over his mouth.

"No, no, not at all. Deogol is a Meek. On occasions, he takes a brainturn that renders him in the state you find him now."

Wow, Santy was goodly indeed at the fibbing. Brychan said, "Ah, yes I remember. Deogol isn't it?"

"Yep."

"Adara. You are safe. My thanks to the OneGreatProvider. Folk are concerned for you."

"Really? Oh."

"We must go quickly. There is chat of sightings of Agro army types coming through the Wilderness."

"I've packed up some stuff for us take."

"Good. Well thought through Addy. Brychan, if you take his top half I'll…"

"He's nowt but a small thing. I'll take him myself," he said, pulled Deogol up and flung him over his shoulder. "Best be quick."

He strode out of the room. We quickly followed. Santy grabbed some neontubes to light our way. "Do not get separated. Do not let Deogol out of sight."

"I won't."

Lights flashed on in quirky zigzags as we

entered the corridor. In the strobe-like light, I saw that it was full of fleeing folk, carrying belongings and lamps of all kinds. They bumped against each other, dropped things, picked them up and got in the way of our descent.

"Calm yourselves. Go to the Auditorium as fast as fast. Do not delay," Brychan said and despite his burden, managed to push his way through the milling bods. We kept up, holding neonglows above our heads.

Brychan held onto Deogol and stepped carefully down the stairs. The hallway brimmed with 'dults and young 'uns eager to flee the blacked out building. They shoved and pushed each other all hasty-like through the great glass doors.

Above the raised voices, shouts of, "Agros, Agros are here."

## Chapter Nineteen
*Havoc In The Hallway*

It was as if a silent explosion had gone off. The mention of Agros caused folk to panic and rush towards the exit. In the darkness, they stumbled and tripped over one another. Flashes of light from torches highlighted the carnage below. Folk fled to the exit in droves. They piled into the doorway as one big blob, causing some to get stuck. Screams and shouts for help were not heeded.

More clambered their way over the bods trapped in the opening. It was a terrible sight to see those stricken being kicked and clawed at by others who's sole intent was to leave. Brychan called out several times for calm and quiet, but not one heeded his wise words. He puffed and panted in an effort to move faster, but the weight of Deogol hampered his progress.

"Let him down, attend to those who need your assistance," Santy said.

"Thanks for that. I will do what I can then come back for the lad." He let Deogol fall into Santy's arms, took her glowlamp, and raced to the exit. He stood in front of the compacted door, held up his hands to dissuade more from attempting to flee. He shouted, "Stop!" so loudly that I thought all the windows in the place would shatter.

Folk did not stop.

Santy turned to me. "Addy, go help. When they see you, they might listen."

Despite hating being in the public eye, I knew she was right. I rushed to where Brychan stood, arms out trying to prevent folk from going around him. My presence did nowt to persuade folk to cease. They merely pushed harder causing Brychan to fall to his knees. I helped him up then turned to the rabble. "Please, everyone stop!" They did not and more bods piled into the exit doors jamming it shut.

"They will kill each other for sure. I am at a loss to know what to do," Brychan said and shakily stood.

I watched the hideous scene before me. Then an idea swooshed into my noggin. Why not sing? I took in a big lungful of air, opened my mouth and let out a sound so piercing and high that all had little choice but to stop, crouch on the floor, and put their hands over their ears.

I ceased my warblings. "If you do not comply with Brychan's wishes, then I will let rip with a higher, louder sound that will quite probably make your guts burst open." My words had some effect. Folk slowly rose and stood facing me. Brychan slapped me on the back.

"Excellent work, Adara." He took the glowlamp, waved it a few times and said, "Stay put. I need some folk to help me prise those that are stuck from the doorway." A silence more silent than before filled the hall. "Will none step forward?"

I did. "I'll help." I heard a shame-filled muttering ripple through the crowd.

"I will too," a male said, then a few more male 'dults stepped forward.

"That will do. Breanna?"

"Yes?"

"Would you keep order whilst we do said task?"

"Gladly, if one kind soul would assist me in carrying Deogol the rest of the way down the stairs."

I ran to her and took my bro's feet. Together we carried him down the steps and laid him onto the floor away from the disruptive bods that wandered about all twitchy-like. Santy waved her arms in the air when folk turned, she spoke loud and clear, "Please stay where you are. Even if you have become separated from kinfolk. Sit still, stay calm. Wait for the exit to be cleared. When it is, I will tell you, but you must not attempt to leave the building until the doorway is clear. Only then will we go, in an orderly fashion."

Eventually, all sank to the floor or steps. They huddled together, mumbling, biting their nails. I turned to help the others free those still jammed in the doorway. Brychan knelt on the floor. He called to those who were in a flesh pile. One by one they answered him. "All alive, but I think some badly injured. Although it would be best not to move them without medi help, under the circumstances we have no choice. We will begin with those on top."

Brychan gestured for me to assist. He gently pulled the arm of a 'dult. The male gasped and fell back into his arms. With the assistance of the other helpers, we made a hominid chain, passing the injured folk one to the other until they reached the ground. Once there, Santy and some other fems, attended to them as best they could with water and soothers.

The rescue became difficult the nearer to the bottom of the pile. We pulled out eight folk that were not too badly harmed, but underneath were four 'dults face down.

Brychan bent low and put his fingers on the neck of one of the two fems that lay motionless. "A faint pulse." He tried the others. "All alive, just.

Santy came over and held out an oxytube. "Give them a gulp on this. It should help to revive them somewhat."

Brychan took it. With my assistance, he placed the cup-like mask over face after face and pumped oxygen into their mouths. It had the desired effect and they began to breathe more easily. Santy aided Brychan in peeling off the stuck together bods until we came to the last one. A male teen I knew. He was sprawled out flat, his head to one side, squashed against the floor. His nose, flattened, oozed blood. I squatted beside him. "Hrypa?" I said it a few times more. On the sixth, "Hrypa?" his eyes flickered open.

"Let me tend to him," Santy said. She took a lightstick from her special kit, shone it into his eyes, across his face, highlighting bruises and cuts on his cheek and jaw. Then she gently pressed her fingers across his bod, put her ear to his chest. "I hear fluid in his lungs. I am no doc or nursey, but have dealt with a similar injury when stationed in the Clonie Zone during their last war with the Agros. I will need light, a sharp needle and as many Steriwipes as you can gather."

I went amongst the seated and procured all the items Santy requested. The sharp needle came from Brychan. He confessed to a pastime of threadweaving and had in his pockets a soft, real cotton purse full of different sized needles.

I said nowt about such a thing being the leisure pursuit of fems, thanked him and handed the pointy sticks to Santy. She chose the biggest one with the sharpest tip, sprayed it with an antiviral spray, and to the gathered horror of one and all, shoved it between his ribs. There was a brief hissing sound then some thin red liquid trickled out. Santy sat back. Hypra coughed.

"Give him a sec to take in some air, then we can lift him."

As Hypra breathed in, I saw his ashen features take on a more ruddy look. Brychan, Santy, and two of the helper 'dults, lifted his limp bod and placed it next to Deogol. I took his hand and despite my ill feelings towards him, squeezed it. He managed to press his fingers in mine. In a faint voice, he said, "Thanks, Adara."

"Not me, it's Santy that saved you."

"Then thanks to your Santy."

Wow, that was the first time since knowing him, that I'd heard him speak in a whisper, never ming give out a, "Ta," to someone. He must be sickly indeed. I smiled at him and let go. He grimaced, went stiff for a sec, then relaxed.

"Are you in much pain?"

"More than I am used to. Will the Firstaiders be here soon?"

"Erm, well…"

"Yes, I'm sure they will. Maybe a bit late, though, but they will be here. You rest now," Santy said and led me away. "Tell them lies, Addy. It serves no purpose to scare them any more than they already are. Hope can keep folk alive. Now we must get those than can walk to the Auditorium."

She took a glowlamp from her pocket, tapped it on the floor and held it above her head. It shone bright and lit up in a halo around her head. For a moment, she looked like a pic I had seen of what the Praisebees called an angel. "The exit is clear, but the injured are littered around the floor. To avoid any more casualties, I would strongly suggest that folk walk slowly in single file to the door. Myself, Brychan, Adara, and the three kind males that assisted in the rescue, will stand in a line holding up torches for you to see your way out. Once in the open, make your way carefully and quickly to the Auditorium. If any decide to make a run for the exit, I will personally take them down. Are we all agreed?"

There came a low murmur of, "Yes, yep. Suppose so." Santy pointed to the exit. I stood by it, a torch held high to illuminate the gap. Next Brychan and the other helpers stood at various points to form a line of dim illumination. It was an eerie sight in this half-light to see folk rise and slowly walk in file to the doorway. They looked like Deogol did when he sleepwalked to his comp. All was quiet except for the fizzing sound that came from the glowsticks, and the sighs of relief that fell from the mouths of residents as they passed through the exit.

When all but the stricken had left, Santy waved to us to gather together. "Thanks for your services. Would you be happy to stay here with the injured that cannot walk?"

"I will stay," Brychan said. He stared at the other 'dult helpers. They nodded.

"Addy, we will see who can travel and take them with us to the Auditorium. Once there, we will procure a Firstaider and their Crisiscar to fetch the others."

We went to the injured and those that

could, stood. We aided them to the front doorway, where they sat waiting for our return. It was goodly indeed that only three bods were unable to make the journey. One was a 'dult fem, one Hrypa, and the other?

"What of Deogol?"

"I will waken him," Santy said. She took me by the arm to where he lay. "The effects of the drug may well be fading from his bloodstream. I will give him a booster. That should revive him enough."

"If not?"

"Then we carry him. I will not leave him alone."

"Do what you must."

Santy took a hypo from her kit and a small phial. She put the needle in, sucked out a goodly quantity of fluid, stuck it into his neck and pushed it all in. It took but a sec for a reaction to occur. Deogol snapped open his eyes, jerked up his head and stared wildly around him.

Santy took his hand. "Deogol, look at me." He did and blubbed. Santy held him until he stopped, then helped him to his feet. He leant against her, his head pressed into her bosom. I gave out a heavy sigh of relief and together we walked towards the exit.

## Chapter Twenty
*Cityplace In Chaos*

The injured rose slowly. I offered my arm to a shaky looking fem. She took it and along with the other residents, we left the building.

It was dark. Darker than it had ever been in Cityplace. The infoboards that cast a bright, constantly changing light, were black. The huge, high walkway lamps, out too. Although it was scary, quite probably dangerous, I took the opportunity of said darkness, to look up at the sky. The storm had passed and it was clear.

The moon shone down and not for the first time in my life upon this planet, I saw her round-mouthed face look down in shock at what was below. Then I saw them. The stars. All twinkly and clustered into geometric shapes that changed into outlines of long dead creatures that once roamed this blighted earth. I felt a nudge in my lower back.

"Not the time or place for stargazing. Do you not hear the rumblings ahead?"

"Nah, too busy witnessing the wonders of the universe."

"Not so great when we are in mortal

danger. Step up the pace if you can," Santy said and walked ahead of me, still clutching onto my bro.

I looked to the fem that hung onto my forearm. "Can you go any faster? Santy thinks there may be Agro threat." She nodded. We travelled less slowly until we reached the central square. What a sight.

The place was dimly lit with outdoor glowlamps that were stuck into the ground around the main walking area. Hundreds of Citydwellers milled about like lost bumbles, holding torches and bags. They swarmed around the plaza tripping and bumping into anything that was unfortunate enough to get in their way. Some ran for a bit, stopped, looked around, ran somewhere else, then stopped. I'd seen dragonflies move in a more coherent pattern than these folk.

The noise they made was dreadful. It was a whining sound like someone had opened the door to a whole room full of hungry bubs, but the sound came from 'dults not young 'uns. I looked at their down-turned mouths and wet faces, and felt ashamed of my fellow dwellers. I shook my head. I could not believe that a fracas with the Agros would turn out well for us.

We pushed through the lamenting lot and

made our way up the steps to the Auditorium, which were strewn with prone bods either blubbing, moaning, or just sitting staring at nowt. Deogol had recovered enough to be able to walk unassisted. He even managed to open the door to the makeshift healingplace.

The scene inside was no better than out. Except it was quieter. Due no doubt to the soothers being liberally administered by doc and nursey alike. They went from bod to bod with pills, water, cushions and blankies. My eyes could not keep up with the speed at which injections were freely given to any who requested them. Typical of Cityfolk to take the easy option. I doubted if half the injured needed such consolation and merely chose to have the meds just because they could.

"Doc!" Santy called. She called a few times more until a slender 'dult approached wearing the telltale white all-in-one suit of a chief medic. "These folk have been hurt during the evacuation of Purityitowers. They have been jammed in a doorway and may have injuries unseen. Also, a Firstaider and their mobile is needed at the block. Two remain, too injured to travel. One most severely, I had to drain his left lung."

The doc brushed his hair from his forehead and blinked. "What? Yes, of course. Take them to the nursey on the stage. As for the Firstaiders, they are out somewhere in the square. Perhaps, Adara, that is you is it not?"

"Yep, me all right."

"A privilege to meet you," he said and held out his hand. I shook it. "If you could go find one, I'm sure they would listen to you and go help those at Puritytowers. I'm afraid with so much confusion and bewilderment, their services are required almost everywhere."

"Shall do. Back in a sec. Deogol?"

"What?" my bro said, unable to look me in the face.

"Will you remain with Santy and not run away?"

"Yep, too tired and limp to go anywhere anyway."

I gave his elbow a squeeze before going out to the square.

My glowlamp stuttered. I was thankful that the templights cast enough brightness for me to see my way around. Folk were huddled in the doorways of the food allocation buildings, which would have been open if things were as they should be.

I wandered the square in search of the Firstaiders. I spied the yellow and red striped suited medi-folk by the fountain, tending to a mum-to-be. I tapped the smaller of the two on the shoulder, she turned. Her brow was furrowed and specks of moisture clung to her eyelashes, upper lip and chin. "What?" she said, her voice all quivery.

"Sorry to be a bother, my name's…"

"Adara. Catcher of Birds."

"Just call me Adara."

"Hey Edwyn, the girly Adara is here."

A stumpy male with face hair, looked at me all wide of eye, gave the sitting preggie fem a soother. "Wow, wow, wow! It is too. Adara, Catcher of Birds."

"It really is just, Adara."

They stood and stared at me like I was a stuffed, died-out beastie, then grinned. I sighed. "I was wondering if you could go in your Crisiscart to Puritytowers? Two badly injured folk could use your services. The doc inside said you would," I added to give more weight to my request. They raised their eyebrows and shrugged. "Well? Folk are in need of your assistance. Now."

"Well 'spose we could. To be frank, most of these lot are just confused. The hurt ones are indoors," Edwyn said. "Come on Arla, let's go."

The Firstaiders shook my hand. Edwyn did not let go and lifted my mitt towards his face. "Look Arla, she really does have six fingers on each hand. I thought it was a jest, but no. Look." She did. I yanked my mutant hand free.

"Folk need your assistance."

"Oh yep, sorry got a bit preoccupied with your fingers."

"Right, so you are now going to the sick that need healing, right?"

"Right," Edwyn said. Both he and Arla walked to their vehicle parked at the bottom of the Auditorium stairs. Arla reached inside the square truck and a red light on top lit up. It spun and sent out flashes of blood coloured light around the square. They got in and sat. Edwyn fired up the motor by pressing a big button on the front of the dashboard. The vehicle made a soft humming noise as he steered it forward.

It was a quickly contraption for sure and I wondered how long it would be before all the seven municipal leckie mobiles ran out of juice; what with the power all but gone. The Firstaiders waved to me as they shot past. I waved back and made my way to the Auditorium.

I entered the building and looked around for my bro and Santy Breanna. She was assisting the doc in doling out meds to the sick. Deogol was standing at the back of the stage by the curfew button. I remembered Lilith and Elijah. The secret tunnels beneath the City. My tum churned, my heart thudded. I was glad when I spotted Santy. I went to her.

"Luck with the Firstaiders?"

"Yep, seemed glad to go and treat deserving cases. Those outside are perturbed nothing more."

"We are lucky indeed. Folk here are not so sick or sore that a bit of med or rest will not cure."

"Then why do you look so concerned?"

"If the Agros do come back, fiercer than before, then we are as good as dead. Folk are not apt for battle. The City S.A.N.T.S. are small in number. Word has gone out for backup. We must wait and see if they will arrive in time."

"About that, could we not use the secret chambers below to hide one and all till the Agros leave?"

"A plan I had considered too. If it comes to that, as a last resort we will."

"Why so hesitant?"

"S.A.N.T.S. have used the tunnels for many orbits to gain free access to Cityplace and beyond, without the Agros knowledge. The more that know of their existence, the more chance that Agros will find out."

"The thought of Agros under the City is a scary thing for sure. Maybe they won't come back."

Santy took my hand and pressed it to her mouth. "Little Addy, you are a buoyant soul to be sure. Look to your bro, see that he comes to no harm."

She pushed me towards the stage and I went up the steps. Deogol looked up as I approached. "They will come back."

"How so certain? Do you know things and will not tell? If you can help us defeat them Deogol, then spill."

He raised the corner of his mouth and snickered. "Defeat the Agros? Us? Nice jest Sis. Look at them. Feeble as newbies. Agros will strike. Cityplace will be no more."

"Really?"

"Fact Sis, fact."

I stared at his face. The Deogol I knew was missing from his kiddle features. A dark, older countenance looked at me now. I could not stand to see him so hurt and angry. I came across all mumsy in the extreme. I could not help but hug my bro. He resisted at first, but my hold was stronger than his struggles. He gave in to my affection and wrapped his arms around my waist. "You are kin, my only bro. I will not let the Agros take you."

"You cannot stop them."

"Can and will, end of."

Deogol pulled away. "Hope so, when it comes to that."

"Up to you bro."

"Is it, though?"

I was about say, "What do you mean?" but my words were cut short by Orva entering the building announcing that Agros were almost at the City boundaries. I grabbed Deogol and we sped down the stairs straight to Santy Breanna.

"Stay here. I will try and get the folk outside to come in. This place if fortified enough to withstand Agro action. There is water and emergency grub in the storage area underneath the stage. The doc is aware of it. He has taken it upon himself to deal with that. Come Orva, help me bring folk in."

Santy and said S.A.N.T. Left. I saw the Firstaiders, Brychan, Hypra, and the others from Puritytowers enter. I put my arm around Deogol, who did not object. Together we walked to the side window by the exit and looked out. Santy and Orva were going amongst the confused folk, steering them towards the Auditorium. I strained my ears to listen for Agro action and heard the sound of many feet stomping. I hugged my bro closer, hoping that those on the outside would soon come in.

They did, quickly, without fuss. I saw several City S.A.N.T.S. send folk towards the entrance. Brychan took it upon himself to usher them to a space inside, attempting to keep a semblance of calm throughout the place. When all had entered, Santy came to us. "Once the doors are shut you will be safe enough. You have some training Addy so I am relying on you to help protect as best you can. Orva and Dreng will be by your side. Make your bro stay within. More will come."

"Are you not staying then?"

"No, Addy. I will defend outside where I am needed most."

"No Santy," Deogol said and grabbed her wrists. "No, stay with us. You have not been a S.A.N.T. for many orbits, you cannot fight the way you used to."

Santy Breanna stiffened and sucked in her

cheeks. "Deogol, a S.A.N.T. is never out of training. I am older it is true, but just as strong and capable as I ever was."

"Please do not go, please."

"Calm now little earwig, Addy will take care of you."

She prised his fingers away, kissed his forehead and touched my cheek. "Be strong," she said and went outside.

## Chapter Twenty-One
*Wobbles Below*

"Adara! I am glad to see ye here, uninjured," Dreng said. His clothes were ruffled and there was evidence from the dust and torn cloth on the knees of his trousers, that he had fallen more than once.

"You have been through much?"

"Nay more than the rest. A few scuffles broke out amongst the crowd. We had to cuff a few noggins to gain order. Yer Santy sent me in to hae my dressing changed."

"How is the wound?"

"Better for the healing spray the doc put on it." He looked at my bro, who was staring at the medi station where a nursey sat tip-tapping upon a comp. "The laddie looks as if he is about to burst."

Indeed, Deogol's eyes were all-a bulging somewhat from the effort at peeking at said device. He bit his lip and walked towards the nursey. "Oy, Bro, stay where I can see you."

"Yeah, yeah, yeah," he said and went to the medi station.

The nursey continued to tap away. My bro stood over her, twitching, no doubt keener than keen to log in and do whatever it is he does on there. She tapped some more then the screen went blank. The nursey growled, poked the keypad several times, when nowt happened, she hit the side of the thing so hard that I thought it would fall off the table it was on. She sat back and folded her arms.

"Huffn' hell. Typical. The thing expires just when I needed it most."

Deogol leant over her shoulder. "I can fix it."

"For real?"

"Yep."

"Then do," she said and stood.

He sat in her place, shoulder twitched, then hit a few keys. The comp whined then started up again.

"You are a wonder. How did you do this?"

"Just know how the thing works. Can I assist in any way in exchange for some time on the comp?"

"Yeah, sure. I need to access a couple of info files, then it is yours."

She narrated some medi stuff I did not understand whilst Deogol tapped. When she had gleaned the info she wanted, she left him to peruse said device on his own.

"He seems content now," Dreng said.

I nodded then turned my attention to what

troubles were occurring outside. Safe in the knowledge that my bro would be going nowhere now that he had his paws on a comp, I walked to the great window by the exit door and looked out. Dreng joined me. After a sec, we both sighed.

The square was all but empty except for the S.A.N.T.S. that stood in each corner. Two were in the centre by the fountain that was shaped like a bluebell. Santy Breanna and Orva stood at the bottom of the stairs leading to the Auditorium.

It was a strange sight to see the plaza so deserted. Most days folk bodded about, sat by the fountain, chatted and the like. Or went to the food provision store, Museum, infoforum, or to work in the seed counting place, school, and municipal buildings. Still don't know what they do there, but folk have to occupy themselves I suppose. Now they were crammed into this room fearing for their lives.

"Dreng, did you hear heavy footsteps a few secs ago?"

"I thought I did and believed the Agro army were all but upon us."

"Strange that all is now quiet. Do you think they have retreated?"

"Does nay sound like something an Agro

would do."

Every part of me wanted to go outside and talk to Santy but knew that if I did, not only would she be furious, but I could end up caught in a fracas. I thought best not to so I bit my fingernails instead.

My hands began to shake. At first I thought I was suffering from delayed shock, but when my feet began to shudder, I knew that something was most severely amiss. I glanced around.

The whole place trembled.

Folk wobbled and grabbed onto each other. Tables bounced or tipped over, and lights crashed to the floor. Dreng touched my arm. We looked outside. The S.A.N.T.S. headed towards the fountain. They too were more than unsteady on their feet.

I fell backwards when a great rumble caused the floor to quake. Dreng helped me up then went to the aid of the medi staff, who were gathering the injured to move them to a safer spot up on the stage area. In case any of the decorative columns were to fall. I went to Deogol. He continued to tap on the comp, seemingly unaware of the rumpus around him.

"Bro?"

"What?"

"What gives?"

"Shhh, go away. I am busy."

I would have given him a slap of being so insolent, but the shuddering that had us all a-quiver, stopped. For a sec, there was silence, then folk began to blabber and fuss. Those not too badly injured noticed that the docs and nursies were securing the sickliest on the stage. A sure indication that something bad was to occur. They began to head for the platform, but there was not the room. Scuffles broke out.

I took it upon myself, being the only one there who was recognisable, to go to the top of the steps and give out some sensible advice. Stuff not that dissimilar from what Santy Breanna said at Puritytowers. I waved my arms about to get their attention, when that didn't work I gave forth a most excellent yell that caused everyone to cease their whining and look to where I stood.

"It's Adara. Catcher of Birds. The girlie from the parade," someone shouted.

"The caller? So it is."

"Look, she really does have six fingers on each hand."

Not again. You'd think with all that was going on, they would have other more important things to talk about. I waved my arms about again, and this time, they listened.

"Folk, please, if you will try to keep as calm as can."

"What is happening?"

"Not sure."

"Is it Agro?"

"Again, not sure."

"Maybe it's a quake?"

"Nah, not likely."

"Then what?"

"Like I said, not sure."

"Hey, Adara?" Drysi's sissy voice.

"Yep."

"What do you want?"

"Erm, for folk to, you know, not all try and fit on the stage. It's somewhat too small to contain the vast numbers that are here. Just before in Puritytowers, a similar incident occurred and did not turn out too well, so if you would…"

"Who put you in charge?"

"Well, no one."

"So why should we do as you wish?"

"Erm, because…I think that…"

"I'm not taking orders from you."

Drysi folded her arms and stuck out her chin like a bub that wants more but cannot have any. I was at a loss as to what to do next as folk began to argue and push each other, when I felt a hand on my shoulder. Mayor Eldwyn. He whispered into my ear, "Just got here. Things are not well without. Below our feet are rumblings I am concerned with. Let me handle these confused folk."

He walked top the top step and coughed most loudly. All turned to him. "Good Cityfolk, it matters not the least if Adara is in charge, what she says is goodly advice. I would recommend that you all stay in the centre of the room where there are fewer objects to crash down. The stage area should be left to those who are injured and need medicare." His words soothed the crowd. Mine, it would seem, only agitated. He turned to me. "Admirable of you to want to help, but I think it best to leave it to 'dults. More authority if it comes from those who have it."

A gentle reprimand that I heeded. My newfound VIP status had quite gone to my head. I smiled thinly.

Dreng came over, slapped my back and gave me a thumbs up sign. I went back down the steps low of head and stood behind Deogol. I peered over his shoulder and tried to make out what he was up to on the comp.

As soon as he became aware of my presence he snapped the down the lid. "Should you be using the comp that belongs to the meds?"

"They said I could."

"What are you doing?"

"Nothing as embarrassing as you."

"Oh, right, guffaw, guffaw, little bro. So tell."

"There is a blabber amongst us."

"Who are 'us'?"

"There is one who knows things of use and has told them to the Agros."

"How do you know?"

"I accessed the Agro site. There is info about the S.A.N.T.S. Also, some underground tunnel system. Does Cityplace have such a thing?"

Huff and then some. "Erm. Well."

"Thought so." He smirked. I wiped my somewhat sweaty face.

"Deogol, this is serious stuff. Find out more."

"That's what I was attempting to do before you halted my progress."

"Who would have this info and leak it?"

"Only folk I can think of would be those in Authority and perhaps a S.A.N.T."

My mind flip-flopped like a dead leaf in the wind. The one last safe haven gone.

Worse, Agros could be under our very feet. I ran from my bro and hurtled towards the exit. Dreng stopped me by flinging out his arm, catching me in mid - flight. I wriggled from his grip. "I must go to Santy and give her some important info."

"Nay it is safer in here."

"No, it is not, that is what I must tell her."

'Nay. Stay put. My job is to keep ye safe and unmolested."

"Under the circumstances, I believe your job is invalid."

"Until given instructions otherwise, I will continue to carry out my duties."

He stood in front of me and every time I stepped to the side to escape, he blocked my way. His loyalty to his assignment was admirable, however, the impending threat of Agros swarming up from the caves below like giant malicious ants, negated his heroics in the extreme. "Listen Dreng, if I give forth some secret info, will you let me pass?"

"That would depend on the info, lassie."

"Well duh."

"Tell and I will decide."

"Fine, fine. Deogol has discovered that the Agros have…" I stopped in mid-sentence. A thought occurred to me that if there was a blabber, it could be anyone with access to

Authority info. Even Dreng. "They have a new way of getting into Cityplace without our knowledge."

"What? How?"

"Erm, not really sure."

"That is the top secret stuff ye need to tell yer Santy?"

"Pretty much." Now, if he were the widemouth, then he would let me go for sure. I waited for him to answer. He screwed up his eyes, wiped his chin and shook his head.

"Nay, not good enough. That info is redundant. My guess would be that those outside would work out Agro infiltration from another source if they do nay attack in the expected way."

"Please let me go."

"Nay," he said and stood before me like a tree. "Okay Dreng, what if I were to tell you a real secret?"

He bent close. I kneed him in the nads then legged it to the exit. I flung open the door and raced to where Santy was chatting with the other S.A.N.T.S. "Santy, Santy!" She turned 'bruptly. I rested my hands on her shoulders.

"Easy Adara, what gives?"

"Deogol," I said, panting heavily.

"Is he gone?"

"No, he has discovered that Agros know about the tunnels."

Pulling away, she put her hands on her cheeks. "That would explain the rumblings below."

"What are we to do?"

She motioned for the City S.A.N.T.S. to gather around her. I walked over, but she waved me away. I stood apart from them, so could not hear what they discussed.

There came a kaboom from the direction of the Auditorium. The S.A.N.T.S. turned as one bod and ran for the place. Santy took my arm and we too legged it. Orva was the first to arrive at the top of the steps. She threw open the door. We followed her in.

What a sight!

Folk lay on the floor bruised and cut. Tables and chairs were upturned, there were cracks in the walls, ceiling and vast columns. Smoke billowed up from fissures in the floor and the back of the stage area. Docs and nursies carried the injured to ground level.

I strained to see Deogol. Santy rushed past me. She threw furniture this way and that searching for my bro. I went amongst the crowd, who were screaming and crying.

Eventually, I found Dreng slumped against a column. He had a cut on his forehead. Blood slid from it and his nose. I knelt next to him. "Dreng?" His eyes flickered open and he put his hands over his nethers. I smiled, he did too.

"Glad ye are not hurt."

"Wish I could say the same. Can you move?"

He nodded and I helped him up. It was not easy having one of his size lean so heavily upon my arm. I tottered a bit and almost fell when he pushed his full weight on my shoulder in order to stand. He wiped the blood from his face. I handed him a wipe from my pocket. He cleaned his big mitts, looked around for a sec then threw the soiled cloth onto the floor. All my instincts as a Citydweller, urged me to pick it up and dispose of it in a correct location. Nope. Things were changing. I was too. I left it there and felt oddly good.

"Is it Agro?"

"Yep, think so."

"Do ye know where they have come from?"

I felt ashamed that I thought he could be the blabber and told all that I knew. Dreng took a step back. "Some secret. Not surprised ye were loath to give it out. I must go and help." Without looking at me, he strode into the mass of bods that scrambled and stumbled around the room.

I lengthened my neck and saw Santy hug a wriggling Deogol. I pushed through folk until I came to them. Santy let go of my bro with one arm and used it to pull me close. She squeezed us both until we squeaked, then let go. "No one is safe here. It sounds as if the Agros are blowing up the tunnels after they have come through them."

"Why would they do that?"

"So that we cannot escape."

"Santy, I am a-feared," Deogol said and clung onto the medicomp.

"We must leave. Now."

"To where?"

"Goldenagehomes?"

"Erm, what?"

"It is far away from the hub of things and has its own medicare centre. The last place the Agros will think to look."

"Don't think the oldies are going to be too keen."

"Don't 'spose they will."

I looked at the sadly folk all fearful and brutalised. They lived such soft lives. This turmoil was for sure, unsettling. My gut twinged. I moaned. Then I felt a tab being pushed into my palm. "It will help quell the cramps," Santy said. I swallowed it down and waited for it to soothe my pulsating innards.

"There are over a five hundred bods here and who knows how many more frightened residents will come from the other side of town. Goldenagehomes is of a largeness to be sure, but all these folk will cram it to capacity."

"It will be cramped, but for a short while only."

"Hope so."

Orva waved to us from the top of the stage. Santy went to her and they became engrossed in some sort of deep in conversation. After a few more secs of furrowed-brow chat, Santy came down. "We need the mayor to gather folk together."

"He could be anywhere."

"Give one of your piercing shouts to call him forth."

Standing on tiptoe, I opened my gob and coughed. Too much muck floated around the room for me to get a clean lungful of air. Santy handed me an oxycan. I sucked from it. This time, I was able to shriek and get the attention of one and all. The folk ceased their bewailing and turned in our direction.

When all was quiet Santy said, "I do not need to tell you that this place is no longer safe. We must go to Goldenagehomes. Take whatever you can. Make your way there as soon as. Is Mayor Eldwyn here?"

"Yes, I am," he said and pushed his way through the crowd.

"Mayor, goodly indeed to see you are unscathed." He was too. Not a speck of dust or slight scratch about his bod. I thought it oddly, but well, he was the mayor and this was not the time to dwell on such matters. Although, he did give me a look quite dark before straining his neck to search for something, or someone.

"Do you require my assistance?"

"Yes. Do you have transport available to take those that cannot walk?"

"Indeed, yes, of course. I have my own large Limo. I will drive them myself."

"A noble gesture to be sure."

Also, redundant. He would have been more use here. His quickness to leave this place was suspish.

"It is the very least I can do, given the circumstances." He addressed the panic-stricken folk. "Please wait for the sick to be organised for transportation. Then go to the safety of the Oldie sanctuary. I shall go next with those that need the least care. The Firstaiders and docs to take the more sickly in any vehicle they have. I take it a S.A.N.T. or two will accompany those on foot?'

"To be sure. I myself will do the honours with the aid of one more," Orva said. Dreng nodded and stood beside her.

I wondered why Santy did not volunteer. I gave her a quizzical look. She leant close to my ear. "I must stay and keep back the Agros. You take care of Deogol."

"Why must you stay?"

"I know their tactics better than anyone here. Go, go to your bro, comfort him." I squeezed her hand and went to Deogol. He tried to go to her, but she was already at the top of the stage with the other S.A.N.T.S.

## Chapter Twenty-Two
*Irked Oldies*

There was a tap on my shoulder. I turned my head. Orva and Dreng stood beside me.

"Glad that you are to accompany us."

"I still hae nay been instructed otherwise, lassie."

I laughed. Deogol frowned and said, "You do realise that your so-called assignment is now void, under the circumstances."

"Ay, laddie, your sis said as much too. It wi just my jest," Dreng said and ruffled his hair.

My bro gave him a stormy look and backed away. "I do not enjoy contact with others apart from my immediate family."

"Sorry, my mistake. Will nay do it again."

Coughing to get rid of the awkwardness, I pointed at the docs and nursies as they ushered out the very sick. "I guess we should be getting to Goldenagehome, now that the poorly are out."

"Indeed," Orva said. "Let us go."

We walked towards the front door. The rest came too. I became uneasy at being followed so close-like by so many, and feared that they would panic and rush for the door just like they did in Puritytowers. Thankfully they did not and we went outside into the darkness that seemed so strange. Once in the open folk began to murmur and jostle. Some activated lightsicks, others simply complained about the injustice of it all. Drysi's whiney voice floated through the rest. "Can't I go home. I want to get some clean clothes to wear?"

"Yep, I would like to wash before we go any further. All this dirt must be causing some kind of germ warfare on our bods."

I did not know who said those words, but they caused a commotion that spread through the crowd. Cries of, "If the Agros don't get us, disease will."

"Another plague will be on us before we can do anything to prevent it!"

Orva looked to me and rolled her eyes, then turned to the almost panic-ridden lot. "May I have your attention? Please, could you listen?" The high-pitched murmuring and shuffling stopped. "Do not be fearful of the muck that is attached to you. I assure you it will wash off and all will be no worse for it being there. So, please, no more lamentations. Agros may be upon us in a heartbeat. We must go now. Follow me. Keep my pace, then we should reach

Goldenagehome in good time. Those with glowsticks keep them held high. Right?"

There came a mass of loudly hissing sounds as many pulled on the cord that lit their glowsticks. Orva waved and pointed forward. "Off we go," she said and we marched. Both she and Dreng keeping the rhythm of our steps. "One, two, three, four. One, two, three four, one, two, three, four." On we tramped mimicking their counting. Across the Centralplaza, past the border guards, through Citypark, until we reached the outskirts of Cityplace.

"All halt!"

All did.

"I must ask you to be quite silent. I will enter first and state our situation. When all is ready I shall call you forth. Please do not enter until told. These oldies are of advancing years, a shock such as this may cause unnecessary harm."

A general whisper of consent wafted through the line of folk. Orva walked over to the entrance gates of Goldenagehome. She pressed the entrancecom and a crackly voice said, "What? Who's there?"

Orva put her mouth close to the com device. "Orva, from the Special Army of the New Territories."

"What does a S.A.N.T. want all the way out here?"

"The City is in trouble. Agro assault. We have been evacuated from the place."

"Are we to leave too?"

"Well, no."

"Then what do you want?"

"We have evacuated to here."

"What?"

"Will you let us in?"

"I don't think so young 'un."

"May I talk with someone in authority?"

"You are."

"I mean, a staffy or med personnel?"

"Go away." The com crackled then went silent.

"That went well," I said.

Standing straight, Orva turned to us. "Okay then. Did anyone hear or recognise the oldie I spoke to?" No response. "Fine. Adara, your Greatgrangran is here is she not?"

"Yep."

"Maybe you could try and get her to come speak with me?"

"I can try, I suppose," I said and pressed the com button. Nowt. I tried a few times more. An angry voice spurted out.

"Why haven't you gone?"

"Oh, hi, hi, my name's Adara."

"Catcher of Birds?"

Huffin' hell, not again. "Yes."

"The girlie in the square?"

"Yep."

"You're going to bring us meat aren't you?"

I was about to say something noble, like, "No huffin' way," and "do not ask again," when Orva poked me in the arm."

"Say yes."

"What? No, nadder. I will not bring the birdies for these mean, Carnie-like oldies. I won't."

Orva let out a huge sigh and Dreng put his hand over his mouth to stifle a snigger.

"Lie. To get us in."

"Oh, right. Will do." I leant nearer the com. "Well, if you let us in, I might just call forth the birdies."

"Really?"

"Really."

There was a muffled bit of chat, then the com crackled and the oldie spoke, "Just you."

"What? No. It has to be all or I won't come in. No meat for you."

Another pause followed by quiet convo.

"You're a sly one."

Orva poked me again. "Call forth your relative."

"Can you get my grangran, please?"

"Amranwen? I'll see if she's available."

This time, Orva patted me on the back instead of poking it. "Good work."

Whilst we waited by the gates, I took a quick peek around. I'd never been here. As far as I knew only oldies abided. The staff came and went, and folk like my grangran, pretty much got on with things until they expired. I looked around, up and along the high concrete wall that enclosed the place, and let out a longly sigh.

What a fortress it was. The only way in or out was through one large, metal gate that we stood behind. I put my hand on it and shook. It was firm all right. Thick and solid. I was glad, for it would take quite a blast in order for it to tumble. I'd always wondered what lay behind these high, impenetrable walls. My guess was that they were constructed on the single storey side to best suit the stiff-leggedness of those that lived there.

Folk began to fidget and whine.

Orva folded her arms, my bro yawned. The com cackled to life. I heard the voice of my grangran. "Addler, they say you are here with many Cityfolk?"

"Yep."

"Agro assault in full swing then?"

"Pretty much."

"How many outside?"

"More than five hundred."

"Yikes. More will come no doubt?"

"Possibly."

"Well, I'll let you in, but if there's any trouble we will expunge one and all."

"We will be goodly I promise." I turned and gave the thumbs up sign. They all cheered. Then I put my ear back to the com.

"I said, are you going to call forth meat?"

"I'd really rather not given the situation we are in."

"Ah now, that's a shame. I ate it once when I was a kiddle. A birdybird fell at my feet all dead. Ma picked it up and brought it in. We didn't know what to do with it so she accessed some info from bygonedays site, which mentioned it should be cooked, so she put it in the waveoven."

I shuddered. "What did it taste like?"

"Plop. I don't think she cooked it right or something, it exploded in the device and she scraped the bits off. It stank too."

"Always enjoy your tales Grangran, can we come in now?"

"What? Oh yes, but not in one great glob."

"Rightly so."

Orva turned to the gathered Cityfolk.

"Families, get into groups. I will allow twenty at a time to enter. When you do, abide by the criteria meted out to you by those that reside here. Do not question, or otherwise annoy the residents, if you do we will be forced to leave. Be ready."

There was a general murmuring and shuffling of position. Then when it appeared that folk were ready, Orva pressed the com button. "We are primed for entry." The huge gate made an unimpressive click sound and both massive doors swung inwards.

What a great place. No wonder the oldies didn't want to share. There was a long curved gravel path lit by sunken solar lights that led to the main entrance. A bright orange sign that said, 'Goldenaghomes' flashed above the glass-panelled wooden door. On either side of the walkway were small ball-shaped bushes that gave off a fresh, grass-like scent. To the left and right of the main building, which had a long sloping red roof, were row after row of goodly sized abodes. They were of wooden construction with similar angled tops, and were adorned with solar panels that looked like they were directly connected to the huts. No doubt to give them individual power.

Greatgran Amranwen emerged from the entrance and greeted us on the metal ramp that took over from the pathway. Behind her stood two tall oldie males holding walking canes like weapons. A not so ancient fem appeared from inside, and came over to us. "Right then, these folk can stuff themselves in our communal area. The building you are staring at. There's foodprepfacilities, places to plop and wash. Also vidscreens and comgames, so the young 'uns can amuse themselves and not cause trouble."

"Many thanks for sharing your splendid home with us," Orva said and gestured towards the folk still tramping through the gates.

"Those Agros are nowt but trouble. You S.A.N.T.S. had better send them off quick."

"We will do our best. How many can you take in the Medicentre?"

"You have wounded?"

"Yes, several."

"Oh, well, I see. Not sure about that."

"The mayor himself is transporting some of the more severely injured."

"Oh, the mayor? Well, I think we can accommodate those unfortunate enough to have come a cropper. The centre is behind this place. Access is via the pathway on the right."

"I will stay outside to await the arrival of the others with your directions," Orva said and stood to one side.

The not-so-old fem peered at the throng and smacked her lips together. "Right. You may enter," she said gesturing towards the entrance. The two oldie males stood either side of the door. Dreng nodded and family after family moved towards the door. The oldie males held their sticks across the entrance. They lifted and dropped them like an automated barrier each time a bod walked in.

I stood with Deogol and Orva, watching folk pile into the spacious building. I did not recognise many of those that passed by, except for Drysi and Hrypa. He was bandaged up, but looked much better than the last time I saw him. Pretty much recovered, judging by the way he was not shouting and hanging onto his ma like a bub. I caught his eye, but he quickly turned away without uttering a word. What a weakling. Ungrateful Wolfie.

Drysi, her dress all torn and mucky, pushed her way through the crowd. She faced me. "I need to use the cleansingplace right away. Look at me, I'm filthy, I can't bear it. Who knows what kinds of germs or killer bugs I have inhaled. I could get sick and die."

If only, I thought. "Hi, Drysi, 'fraid it's not up to me to decide who gets firsties on that kind of thing."

"Who does?"

I shrugged. She let out a, "Fffffsh," and strode into the building. Greatgrangran took my arm and led me away. Deogol stayed put by Orva's side.

"How bad is it?"

"Very and then some. I reckon it has only just begun."

"Could the Agros come here?"

"Hard to say. We don't know how many there are."

"I suppose we'll just have to wait and see."

"'Sppose."

There was a loud honk. I guessed it was the mayor. I glanced down the path and saw said male's limo and the Firstaiders vehicle glide up towards us. Mayor Eldwyn got out. Grangran greeted him with, "How goes it in the square?"

"More explosions. No sign of Agro as yet.

Nothing else to report."

Orva shook his hand. "The Medicentre is to the right behind this place where all are safely stashed."

"Good, good. Edwyn, Arla, take the sick there."

The Firstaiders poked their heads from their vehicle and nodded. Then they drove slowly to the place Orva pointed at. The mayor brushed past me as if I no longer existed and entered the communal place, closely followed by the fem and male oldies. Grangran took my hand. "All we can do is wait. Come inside. You look like you are need of some some grub."

"Nah, you take Deogol. I'll stay here. Keep a look out."

"That may be difficult when the gate is shut."

The thing closed with a mighty bang and it did indeed block the view. Not that I could see much of anything, except darkness and dirt tracks. Greatgrangran went to Deogol, who was standing next to Dreng at the foot of the entrance slope. She touched his elbow and led him indoors. Just like that.

Orva tilted her head in the direction of the door. "Go in Adara, I'll stay with Dreng and keep a lookout."

"Nah, rather be outside. Don't relish the notion of snuggling up to those crybubs inside."

"Everyone is scared. They should be."

"Are you?"

"Yep."

"Gulp, then."

"We are as safe here as anywhere in all of Cityplace. How those that remain will cope, I do not know. But there may be severe casualties before the moon is done with us."

I looked up at the sky. Clouds obscured the pretty stars and all was black. Except for the flash of bright light, that shot up from the direction of Centralplaza. A low boom accompanied the second burst of light. A louder bang caused folk to spill out into the courtyard.

"It's started," the mayor said and went back inside. Everyone followed.

I shivered.

## Chapter Twenty-Three
*The Blabbermouth Is Revealed*

Orva pulled out a shortcomdevice from her legpouch and took to tapping many buttons. She shook the thing, tapped again, lifted it to her ear, then said, "Hi, hi. Breanna?" several times before putting it back with a huff.

"I'll gae to the square, see what's what," Dreng said.

Orva stayed him with a 'brupt forefinger command, "No. You know our orders are to remain here and protect as best we can in case they make it this far."

"All the same."

"Go inside and calm folk. That is what we must do for the best."

He opened his gob, closed it then plodded up the slope into the building.

"Will they come?"

"It depends on your Santy and the others."

I walked to the gate and put my throbbing head against it. It was cool and the coldness of the steel soothed the aching somewhat. Then I thought the thrumming inside my nonce had escaped. For there came a faint pounding that sounded as if it were coming from the base of the metal barrier. I lifted my head away, knelt down and pressed my ear to the ground. The thudding became louder and higher up.

"Is someone knocking?" Orva said and came up beside me. She too listened. "Folk outside."

"What if they are Agros?"

Orva pressed the entrancecom. It buzzed and a voice said. "Praise the lord! Praise the BabyCheesus too. Please, will you let us in?" I recognised that nasal voice. Lilith. I turned to Orva. She narrowed her eyes.

"Thought they were done for. Oh well, best give them sanctuary," she said with a look quite guilt-filled. Coughing loudly, she nodded in the direction of the gate. "I'll just go and…" without finishing her sentence, she raced indoors. A few secs passed and the gate opened revealing the two Praisebees I'd been locked up with.

"Let us in quick. They are hot on our heels," Lilith said rushing past me. Elijah limped through. The gate slammed shut. He was hard to look at. Thinner than any I had ever seen. The skin on his face was stretched so tight that I feared the bones would split through and show themselves. His clothes all tattered and filth ridden, hung from his emaciated bod like a bub dressed in 'dult attire. I held out my hand and he stared at it with dead eyes.

"Elijah? It is Adara. Do you recall who I am?"

He lifted his gaze and blinked. "They left us alone in that place."

"Come, let us go inside." I reached for his arm, but he recoiled in fear.

"No, never going indoors again." He sank to the ground and covered his face with his hands.

I noticed his fingernails were bloody and torn as if he had been scratching a hard surface for quite some time. One digit appeared much shorter than the rest. I knelt beside him, took off my Synthbag, pulled out a bottle of water and a ricerusk. I broke the disc in half, remembering how he reacted to food and drink the last time, and touched his fingers. Yeuk. Dead man's hand. Cold, bony and damp.

He lowered his mitts. I offered him the goodies. He snatched the stuff from my grip and I had to pull the water away from his parched lips when he gulped too fast. He took the hint and nibbled but a tiny piece of rusk before taking another bite. I gave him the water and he sipped it slow.

"How did you escape?"

"Agro troops, or whatever they are, found us and took us with them to the surface. All is bad back there. May the Lord have mercy on their souls."

"How did you know to come here?"

"Fem S.A.N.T. saw us and bundled us away from the onslaught. She told us where to go. Good job Lilith was of sound mind to take it all in. I was confused so."

"Santy I bet. Who wins?"

"No one. Wars such as these can never be won. Know this," he said and gestured for me to lean in, I did. "They are close behind. I heard their breath on my neck. Felt their words of hatred in my ears and mouth."

I did not know what to make of his food-starved babble, so just helped him to his feet. I walked with him to the entrance, but he refused top go in. "I will linger here. I would rather die in the open."

"You won't die. At least not just yet."

"Really?"

I heard something, not unlike foot stamping and looked to the main gate. I gasped. It was open. Before my disbelieving eyes, four helmeted Agros marched up the pathway. I grabbed Elijah and pulled him inside. "Danger!" I cried.

Swifter than a shooting star, Dreng and

Orva ran to the door and pressed themselves against it. A forest of faces turned to me. "Agros! Agros are here!"

Folk scattered.

Urged on by Orva, I helped Elijah hobble through the mayhem to sit in a chair. After taking it from a perfectly healthy juve by kicking his shins until he budged. The sound of heavy pounding caused folk to scream and scuttle to the nearest wall. They fell to the ground and hid behind tables or vidscreens. How they thought that would help I don't know.

Pushing over chairs and tables, I made my way through huddled bods in search of Deogol, but did not find him. Then I caught sight of Greatgrangran slumped over a small table underneath a window at the far end of the great high-ceilinged room. I raced to her and put my hand on her head. She gave a faint moan. I heard a high-pitched chuckle.

Lilith.

She was standing next to the mayor, a piece of bread in one hand and a great hunk of cheese in the other. Where she procured such a rarity from I did not know. Milk curd being only issued once an orbit and not in such sizable chunks. I headed towards them.

"Deogol, have you seen him?" The mayor

scuttled sideways by way of response.

Lilith giggled harder then rammed even more yellow stuff down her sneering gob. I slapped the cheese from her hand. "Have you seen my bro?"

She scrambled on the floor and picked up the grub. "I don't know who you are talking about."

"Filthy liar." I turned to the mayor. "Have you seen him?"

He looked at the window. I hurtled to it. It was ajar. I put my head outside. Too dark to see anything. I pulled my head back in and ran about the room calling his name. Orva came to me. "Adara, what gives?"

"Deogol is not here. The window is open and the mayor…"

"The mayor?"

Through gulps, I managed to splutter out, "The mayor is acting more than suspish. He and Lilith…" Orva stopped me with a finger to her lips.

"I think our mayor has some explaining to do," she said. We walked to where he stood. He gave us a well-used grin. Orva scowled. "Agros are here. Should you not be safeguarding all in this place?" She grabbed his jacket lapel and pulled him close to her face. "What do you know of all this?"

"Nowt, nothing. How could I?"

Lilith laughed so loudly that Orva released her grip. The Praisebee smirked at us then addressed the huddled masses. In a loud voice, she said, "Tell them about what lies below Cityplace."

"Me? I know nothing of the underground passageways." The mayor slapped his hand across his mouth, went all pale and scuttled away.

I shouted after him. "Where is my bro?"

Lilith laughed again. "Oh, him. Gone to a better place."

The front door burst open sending Dreng stumbling backwards, but he soon righted himself and stood his ground as four Agros stormed in. Orva raced to his assistance. Before the enemy could raise their nasty nail spurting guns, they smacked three of them to the ground. Dreng hurled himself at another sending both 'dults sprawling along the floor.

Something switched on in my gut. An instinctive response to threat. I picked up a broken chair, smashed it against the ground so that only half the metal frame remained, and ran towards the remaining Agro scum.

Slamming the makeshift weapon across his chest, he slumped forward. I hit him twice more on the back. He fell face first to the ground and lay still. Orva and Dreng, having floored their Agro scum, were tying them up. When said foe were well and truly tethered, Orva came to me, stared at the prone Agro and said, "Nicely done." She set about securing him and with the help of Dreng, dragged him to the middle of the room where the other Agros sat.

"More will come, be sure of that," one of the bound said.

"Silence Agro filth." Dreng thwacked him hard across the head.

The male snickered most horribly and I noticed when his lips slid upwards, that his teeth were sharpened. I nudged Orva. "I do not think these are Agros. Look to his mouth." She did. "Carnies."

"You are not Agro," Orva said.

He ignored her words and simply said, "Surrender. If you do, you will be spared."

"Spared what?"

The tethered male grinned. Dreng gave him a smack so hard that he fell sideways.

"There are here to kill us!" Bigmouthed Hrypa's voice ripped through the room like an oldies fart, and caused an outbreak of vocal panic. Orva waved her hands in the air, called for quiet, but it did no good and folk began to head for the exit. I caught sight of Meilyr, the nursey that had been so kind to Grangran when the Praisebees nobbled my coming out ceremony. He was trying to push folk away from the door, but was too nice to use enough force.

"You are strong, give them a proper shove and they will yield," I said.

"Adara, goodly good to see you again. I am afraid that I'm unused to giving out brute in this manner. The old ones complain and nag, but have never given us any trouble, not like this."

"Here, do what I do." I stood in a similar manner as Dreng had in Centralplaza and held up my big mitts. He did the same and when the scaredy ones came forwards, they were blocked by our combined bulk.

"Goodly plan. Many thanks."

My thoughts turned to my bro. As much as I would have liked to stay and aid Meilyr, I could not, so I called to Orva and Dreng. They hurried over relieved me of my duty and l went to my Greatgrangran, who had recovered a little. She was standing by the table she sat at before. I looked around for the mayor and Lilith but couldn't see them.

"He opened the window. They climbed out. Just like that. I reached for him, then all went dark," Greatgrangran said and rubbed the side of her head.

Cowards.

The hubbub abated somewhat as Orva, Dreng and Meilyr soothed the fleeing folk. They shushed them back into the room and set about distributing water and edibles. I turned to Grangran, her face showed signs of upset. Her small eyes were screwed up, her lips twitched and her chin wobbled.

"I will go and search for him, do not fret so."

Greatgrangran wiped her eyes and took my hand. "He is lost Adara. They have him. Ah, more will be taken. More have gone before."

"What are you saying?"

"Remember Aefre?"

"A bit. She came to see Deogol once or twice, then that was that."

"Took."

"Nah, folk would have said something."

"Folk don't care if a Meek no longer abides."

"Not true."

"Did you concern yourself when she stopped her visits?"

I looked at the floor.

"Find him, Adara." She squeezed my

fingers until they hurt and I pulled away.

"I will. I vow most severely."

She put her hand to her shoulder and slipped off her Synthbag. She opened a front pocket and gave me a handful of glowsticks. Then she looked to the ceiling and put her hand in front of her mouth. "Lean in close."

I did.

Pressing her lips almost against my ear, she whispered. "Silly me. I think I was dreaming when first I spoke of Deogol's whereabouts. Fear not, he is not lost. The mayor and that nasty Praisebee fem were eyeballing him, muttering all suspish-like, so I sent your bro to a safe place until you returned. That is where you must go to bring him back. There is a small exit at the far corner of the site. Behind the Medicentre. A thorn bush in a big red pot marks the spot. Tap in the numbers, eight, three, five, eight and it will open."

"To where?"

"The place where the menials abide."

"But it is forbidden to go there."

"I did not take you for a scaredykittle."

"I'm not. In fact, I've sort of been there before."

"Anyway, he isn't amongst them. There is a hole in the ground just before their sector begins. You'll know it by the lightning rod."

"I do know where that is."

"The hiding place is directly below it."

"How do you know of this?"

Grangran chuckled and stepped back. I turned to her and she tapped the side of her nose. "Some of us oldie folk have a need to store certain goodies from other oldies. Things that are hard to come by, that we have negotiated for with folk such as the Ladies. Where do you think your Synthbag came from eh?"

I blinked. Wow! My Greatgrangran was a devious fem indeed. I shook my head and said, "I'd best go get Deogol then."

Orva approached with a solemn look upon her face. "You have news of your bro?"

"Yep. Greatgrangran knows where he is."

"Is he far?"

"No."

"Then you must go to him quickly. If the onslaught becomes fiercer, all will be threatened."

Mebbe folk heard what she said, for some began to shout out about threat, danger and not being safe no matter where they were. Orva sighed, waved her arms to quieten them and said, "Do not panic. We are safe within these impenetrable walls. I have sent

Dreng back to the Centralplaza to see what gives there. Please remain here, stay as calm as you can."

"What are you going to do with those Agros?" Hypra said all whiny-like.

"Firstly, they are not Agros. They are in fact, Carnies doing bad for their bosses. Secondly, I am going to gain valuable info. Now please, eat, drink, stay at ease." Her words caused many more loud whispers. She put her fingers to her lips and the hissy noise ceased.

She stepped down. "Amranwen, is there a place where I can take our hostages and interrogate them?"

"Use the foodprep room, it has a sink and a Firstaidbox."

"Duly noted," Orva said and gave me a soothing smile. She left, hauling the Agros, one-by-one, into the place for eating.

## Chapter Twenty-Four
*The Wonder Of Goldenagehome*

Grangran gave a longly sigh, then coughed and plonked her rear on a chair. My belows began to quiver. I clutched at my tum.

"Got the reddies?"

"Yep."

"Looks like you need to go change your sponge. There is a poo place just inside the entrance hall, left of the door. Do you have sponges? Because if not, you're doomed to bleed all over. Not much need of them in this place. Although, we do have some wee pants that are quite absorbent."

"No ta. I have plenty of said plugs," I said and walked swiftly to the place Grangran mentioned. I opened the door. A soft orange light pinged on. There was a mirror above the washbasin. I caught sight of my face. All covered in muck, scratches and bits of dried blood, I looked more like a Woodsfolk fem that had rolled in mud, than a girlie from Cityplace.

I turned on the tap and out came hot water. I squeezed some softsoap from the wall dispenser and washed my filthy hands and face. Next I dried myself on the plump, white towels that hung over a heated rail next to the plop bowl. I lifted the lid of said receptacle, pulled down my troos and let whatever wanted to, come out. When I had finished and wiped my bot, pulled out my bloated reddy sponge, replacing it with a fresh one, I yanked my pants back up, sighed, washed again and went back to Greatgrangran.

She was fumbling around in her Synthbag when I returned. I touched her shoulder and she looked up. I grinned. "Hi, feeling much better now."

"Look better too. I know what will make you feel even more so," she said and took a bigly bar of Sterichoc from her bag. She unwrapped it, broke it in half and offered said segment to me. "Ta." I put it to my mouth, then paused. I caught Elijah's eye. He was crouched against the wall by the exit, hands clenched together in prayer. He lowered his gaze. I walked over to him. He was muttering some kind of chant and lifted his head when I tapped him on the back.

"Here, eat this," I said and handed him the choc.

"Most kind."

"Nah, just not peckish."

He ate the sweetie thing in one go. I itched

to be free of him, to go find Deogol. Giving him a friendly grin, I turned and went back to Greatgrangran. She stared at me and nodded. "All set?"

"Yep."

"Best slip out the window like those two degenerates."

"About that. Do you think they know of the secret exit you told me of?"

"Wouldn't be surprised. He's a shifty one that mayor."

I became apprehensive. What if they lingered and wanted to do me harm?

Or worse, they knew where Deogol was and had intentions unpleasant as regards to my bro?

"What do you wait for?"

"Nowt."

"Off you go then," Grangran said and gave me a shove with her gnarly fingers. I sucked in my fear. Then, when no one was looking at me, not even Elijah, who was otherwise occupied picking a scab from his arm, I crept to and out of the window.

The darkness made a good cloak for me to make my escape. Once away from the glow of the lights from inside the oldie building, I was all but invisible. The Medicentre was not far and I made my way there quickly.

Making sure I stayed well away from the illuminated pathways and windows. Once past the last lit building, I was plunged into darkness. I cracked a glowstick and held it out. Just a few paces ahead I saw the thorn bush that Greatgrangran told me about.

I hurried over, knelt down, stroked the surface of the pot the bush was in, and felt a raised keypad at the back. I tapped in the numbers eight, three, five, eight. I heard a creaking noise ahead of me. Standing, I saw within the great stone wall, a small, hinged door open. With the glowstick held firmly, I ran to the exit and slipped through. The opening slammed shut.

Nad!

I'd forgot to ask Grangran how to get back in.

Then I heard another bang in the distance. Without thinking, I ran forward towards the minion quarters. They were closer than I thought.

Distinct from other Citydweller abodes, these were single story accommodations, with windows in the roof instead of all around. Santy took us there once to do a sort of recon. It was a playtime thing, thinly disguised as a bit of S.A.N.T. training, so I knew my way around, a bit. I wondered, how much these folk that do all the nasty jobs and lived in relative squalor, fared in all this Agro assault. Then I saw the lightning rod and all thoughts of anything else, except getting my bro, left.

Dashing to the pole, I fell onto my hands and knees and scuffed the dirt around until my fingers touched the indented outline of a large square. A little more probing and I came upon a metal ring lever. I pulled, it opened. Out popped my bro pointing a knife at my face.

"Hi," I said and swatted the weapon from his shaky hands.

"Adara, but I thought…"

"Yep, me. Who else?"

"Oh, no one."

"Did you expect someone else?"

He lowered his gaze for a sec. I felt a hair tingle crawl up my back. "Nope."

"Deogol, Look at me." He did. "Do you tell the truth?" Before he could answer the glowstick stuttered and went out. Then a brighter light shone.

"See? Grangran gave me this excellent torch," Deogol said in a pathetic attempt at changing the subject. He threw it from hand to hand as if it were a toy.

"Give that to me, you are attracting who

knows what attention and giving away our whereabouts."

He reluctantly did, but not after waving it around as if to attract the attention of someone nearby. Grabbing onto the collar of his tunic, I pulled him out of the dark hole. He brushed his troos and grinned. "You should see what the oldies have down there. I swear I have never seen such treasures. Comps, slabs, choc, and other goodies. I ate some. Do you think they'll notice?"

"Oh yeah, for sure. But I don't suppose it will matter just yet, what with all the skirmishing that is going on. I would say, let's get back quick, but forgot to ask Grangran how to access the inaccessible."

My bro grinned wider. "Oh, I know how to open the door. Grangran told me."

I let out a goodly sigh. "Does the hatch lock?"

"Yep." He closed said lid and twisted the handle until I heard a clunk.

"Not very secure."

"Don't need to be Sis, no one knows it is here."

A low boom, boom caused us to look in the direction of Goldenagehomes.

"Come on, quick," I said and together we ran back from whence we came.

When we reached the great wall of the oldie building, a huge column of smoke billowed past us. Carrying with it, a stench of something sweet and sickly. Deogol stopped.

I held the torch high so that we and the wall became illuminated. He looked around for some time. When I glared at him, he fell to the ground all quick-like. He pushed his hands along the bottom of the wall and to my surprise up popped a touch panel like the one on the pot.

"Shine the torch so I can see the pad to tap in the numbers."

I did so and my bro tip-tapped. The small, barely visible door, opened. Then I heard a familiar voice.

"I told you it was best to hide and wait."

What the huff?

Out from the gloom walked Lilith and Mayor Eldwyn. "Indeed Lilith, you are wiser than you look. Do not move, Auger, that goes for you too Meek," he said and shone a light into my bro's face.

"Wa? What did he call me?" Deogol said. His mouth thinned, his eyes narrowed and he clenched his hands into fists. "That's what they called me before they took me to the Decontamination Centre." He spat and walked towards the mayor.

"Stay where you are."

"Or what?" I said and also made my way to the two Agro collaborators.

The floor made contact with my back. The air in my lungs spluttered out. I scrambled to my feet and as I lifted my torch, saw the claw-like mitts of Lilith before my eyes. I smacked them away, she threw herself towards me, I sidestepped, she fell on her face. I placed my foot on her behind. She gave out a fierce screech when I bent down and pulled her head up by the hair.

"Take your filthy heathen hands off me!"

"Not likely, wolfbitch."

She made more ear hurting noises before quieting down. Then said all menacingly-like, "More will come."

"Yeah, yeah, heard that before. Keep it shtum Lilith."

She growled a bit then fell silent. I took my foot away, yanked her arms around her back, and pulled her up.

"Let her go," Mayor Eldwyn said.

"Don't think so."

"Do it. Now!" He held up one of those nasty Agro guns. "I will fire unless you do."

"Go ahead," I said and placed Lilith's bod in front of mine. She wriggled with force, and before I could slap her, thrust her head back sharp, and banged me in the noggin. I staggered backwards, blood streaming from my conk.

"Shoot her Eldy, shoot her."

The mayor raised the gun. I closed my eyes. There was a loud bang. When I did not feel pain, I opened my lids. I blinked and saw Mayor Eldwyn crumple to the ground. Deogol stood over him. He looked at me and dropped the weapon. Before I could take in what the huff was going on, Lilith staggered forwards, grabbed the gun from the ground and pointed it at me.

"Drop it Praisebee, or you will be nestling close to your chum."

I swivelled around. "Santy Breanna."

"Lower your torch Addy."

"Ah, sorry," I said and shone it on Lilith instead.

With a hiss-roar, Lilith lurched forward and grabbed my bro. She held the Agro gun to his head.

"Let us both go. I will not harm the kiddle if you do."

"Drop the weapon," Santy said.

"No." Lilith took the gun away from Deogol's head then pointed it at me. "Let me and the Meek go, or I will kill him and the

Auger."

Faster than a sanitary door spray squirt, Santy threw her special knife at Lilith's mitt. She dropped the Agro weapon, and sank to her knees clutching her injured paw. Deogol raced over to us.

Santy pulled out a restraining tie from her sleeve pouch. She walked over to the simpering fem, pulled out her knife, causing more wailing, wrapped the cord around her wrists and yanked her to her feet. Then she took a mediswab from her sleeve pouch, placed it on the wound her blade made in the Praisebee's flesh, and pushed her towards the door in the wall.

"More will come."

"Be still and quiet." Santy tightened the restraint. Lilith grimaced then grinned.

"Eldy contacted them you know. He was the one who let us in. His idea to give me the knife. He bargained with the Agros, they want something you have."

"Ta for spilling Lilith, but pretty much figured that bit out. What with him trying to kill me and all."

"He wasn't going to kill you."

"Really? Looked like that was exactly what he was going to do."

Lilith smirked, cocked her head to one

side and stared at me. "They wouldn't let him. Plans for you girlie."

Santy snorted and shoved Lilith towards the entrance.

"Hey, what about Mayor Eldwyn?"

"Let the clean up minions deal with that garbage."

## Chapter Twenty-Five
*A Different Threat*


When we returned to the oldie place, all was relatively calm. Except for Elijah, who on seeing Santy shove Lilith into the room, shot out of his chair next to Grangran and hid under a table. There were more medifolk than before too along with S.A.N.T.S. the two Firstaiders, and Meilyr, all busy bandaging folk and the like.

Orva entered from the foodprep room. Her mouth was a slit, her eyes too. On clocking our presence, she lost the look of worry and smiled. "I see you found more than your bro, Adara. Good to see you Breanna," she said touching Santy on the shoulder. Lilith tugged at her restraint and gave out a low growl.

"Silence, Agro collaborator. Orva, do you have a room to stash garbage?"

"Indeed I do." Said S.A.N.T. nodded in the direction of the foodprep room and took hold of the Praisebee's bonds. "I'll leave her with the other Agro wannabees," she said and dragged a hissing Lilith to said place.

We heard much scuffling before all went quiet, then Orva returned.

"How goes the battle?"

"Better than before."

"Much better. In fact it is all but finished, ye will be glad tae hear."

We all turned as Dreng entered. He was grubby and scuffed about, but walked steady with had a swagger that would suggest the battle was won.

"What? Is it over?"

"Aye, it is, Deogol." My bro cast his eyes down. I swear he looked disappointed. Nah, my imagination was racing and then some. Dreng continued, "Agros make a lot of noise to be sure, but they sent too few to make much of a dent in our defences."

"They are not Agros, Carnies. Paid in meat to do Agro nastiness," Orva said.

"Carnies. Aye, that would make sense. I thought they crumbled too quick."

"Will more come?" Elijah's high voice cut through our agitated convo. He stood before us, shivering and pale.

"Maybe, laddie, but this time, we are ready. Word has gone forth, the Wilderness S.A.N.T.S. are primed."

Elijah stepped forward all wobble-legged. He stared at Dreng and Orva. Breathing in a stutter breath, he said almost in a whisper, "You left us to die in those chambers. May god have mercy on your soul."

"My what?"

"The thing that their god gives you when you are born. Apparently it goes back to him when they expire," I said.

"Oh, well then, thanks."

"I don't think it was meant to flatter."

"How could you do such a thing?"

Orva faced the trembling Elijah. "Look, you and that other Praisebee were a danger. We did not, in fact, leave you down there to die. We left you down there with provisions, so that we could come back and free you when the time was right."

"How long?"

"What?"

"How long before the time would have been right?"

"I don't know for sure."

He held out his left hand. The tip of his little finger was missing. It oozed yellow pus. "Lilith chewed it off whilst I was out of it." He waved it under Orva's nose. She winced, turned her head and called to Arla.

With a quick glance at the disfigured digit and his scrawny bod, Arla, swift as a spider's bite, jabbed a hypo into his arm. She blocked his fall with her chest and shook her head. "Sheesh, there's nowt to the poor thing."

Meilyr came over and picked him up as though he were a tot. "Poor lad. I'll take him to the Medicentre to get treated." He hoisted Elijah up and over his shoulder then carried him out. Arla cast her eyes to the ceiling and followed them.

"He's had much to cope with," Deogol said.

"How would you know?"

"The look of fear in his eyes, Sis."

"I see that look on many other folk."

"Not as much as he."

Santy exhaled loudly. We knew to cease our chat. She beckoned for us to move away. We did and went through the entrance hall out into the dark. The bangs and whooshes were no more. Clouds that had been heavy were gone. A half moon that looked like a crooked smile in the starless sky shone a thin light upon us three.

"There is something in the air that makes me anxious. Agros sending inferior warriors to shake folk up? They want us broken and weak."

"So that they can send in real troops to finish the job?"

"What job, Addy? What do they really want?"

"I thought it was to free the Praisebees, but they have. So now what? All this for Deogol?"

"Nah, they do not want me. What for eh?"

Furrowing her forehead and raising one eyebrow, Santy looked at my bro. "How did they get in so easily? Are our perimeter defences so puny that in less than two moons loony Praisebees and Carnies pretending to be Agros, have gatecrashed us? How did the fence that is hooked to alarms, manned at all times, stop being live and guarded? After all, Cityplace was built specifically to keep any outsiders coming in without special invitation."

I shrugged. "Yep, it is a puzzle all right. I mean, how can we fight back when any folk who choose to can saunter in and do what the huff they like?"

"At least the City Guards and Wilderness S.A.N.T.S. are here now to man the fences. Ah, it is all Mayor Eldwyn's doing. What he hoped to gain from this I do not know."

"Perhaps he wanted meat? Perhaps he was a Carnie too? He wanted Adara to bring down the birdies."

I turned to my bro. "Goodly thinking. You may be right."

A chilly wind stirred up some dusty earth.

It swirled around our bods and up into the air. We watched it blow away towards the Minion quarters and beyond to the perimeter fence. Not such an oddly thing for sure, but something in the way it moved all uniform, full of purpose, made us shoulder twitch.

"Are we safe?"

"I thought so, Deogol. Go inside." Santy turned to me. "Something is not right. Inside Deogol, now."

My bro frowned so deeply that I thought his brow would drop off.

"No, I want to stay here."

"Go. Sit with your grangran little earwig. Now is not the time to rebel. Stay with her and do not leave this complex."

"But…"

"Deogol, do as I say."

"Wa? Huffin' hell," he said and slunked away into the main building. He paused at the entrance, looked over his shoulder and narrowed his eyes. I did not care for the expression on his face. He snorted and went inside.

A low whiz-bang sound came from far away. A cloud of smoke rose high into the sky. "When will they cease? Does that cloud come from Centralplaza?"

Santy shook her head. "Looks likely. We

must end this, somehow. We must."

I put my hand on her arm, she gave me a sad smile.

"Hey, hey, hey" Orva called and walked briskly towards us. Her face was pale. Her mouth twitched and she grimaced as though she had swallowed something nasty. "I have received news. They have let incendiaries scatter around Cityplace. These devices have tore and slashed and stung like hornets. Inside residential buildings, Breanna. They came into folk's homes. Not enough to strip the Seedbank bare it would seem. They think they have taken all our seedless, but they have not. They merely robbed us of our excess."

"There is much carnage without?"

Orva nodded. "There will be much to repair."

A large stone fell at my feet, then another. "What the huff?" I said and saw more rocks hurtling through the air. They fell near to the outer gate. One struck the S.A.N.T. guard on the cheek. He staggered forward and Santy went to him. His wound spouted profusely. She pointed at the Medicentre. He stumbled off and the stone throwing ceased.

"Who is doing is?"

"Dunno," I said and looked around, but

saw nowt. Then we heard a crashing sound.

"Did ye see her?"

We turned.

Dreng raced down the ramp. His mouth bled, his right hand between thumb and forefinger too. "That Praisebee wolfwhore, has escaped."

"What? How?"

"She said she wanted tae relieve herself so I untied her bonds. She back nutted me, hurled the chair she was sitting on through the window. When I grabbed her, she turned and bit me," he said and held up his tooth marked mitt. "Did ye see her?"

"Well, she won't get far, the place is guarded on all sides." As soon as Santy said those words, the main gate opened and a figure darted through it dragging another familiar bod. Then it closed shut.

"Huff and nad. Deogol!"

"I'll gae bring her back," Dreng said and ran to the gate. He tried to open it, but it was sealed shut. "Tell them within tae open this thing now!"

"There is no need to," Santy said. "We will use the secret exit. Come on Dreng. Addy, go inside until we return."

"No. I can be of use."

"How?"

"Dunno," I said and hung my head.

"We do not have time to argue. Orva, keep vigilant. Stay by the gate."

"Done. Come back soon."

"Come on. Let this be the start of your S.A.N.T. training. Pursuing the enemy."

I near jumped with glee. I did not, though. Instead, I followed Dreng and Santy to the back of the complex and the secret opening. A S.A.N.T. guard stood watch. Dreng whispered something to him and he turned his back whilst I tapped in the numbers Grangran had given me. The wall became a door and we quickly went through it into the grey dark before the sun rises.

We raced around the complex to the outside gate where Lilith had taken Deogol too many secs before. Santy shone a torch upon the ground looking for tell-tale footprints. "Ah, too many tracks to know who's are who's. Where would she go?"

I scratched my noggin. "The Auditorium. The secret tunnels to escape?"

"Good thinking."

We Turned right and swiftly headed towards Cityplaza. As dawn approached, the sky became brighter so there was no need for artificial illumination. As we neared, I thought I heard my bro and called his name.

"You see him?"

"No. Santy, did you hear?"

"No, Addy."

"I swear I heard Deogol."

"From where?"

"Dunno."

Santy sighed. We ran full pelt to the place and stared at the once clean and uniform square. Now it was little more than rubble. There was debris everywhere. A great hole in the side of the Auditorium spewed out clouds of dust. The fountain was a heap of broken cement and the great infoboard, nowt more than a twisted metal frame with bits of melted plassy hanging from it. Thousands of spent ammo, and those golden nail slugs littered the floor. The provision store and other buildings looked intact except for a few broken windows. The seedle bank doors were gone.

"What a woeful sight," Santy said. All slow of foot we walked amongst the ruin as moontime ended.

The sun shot down daggers of brightness that illuminated patches of devastation. Split walkway stones jutted upwards like mini volcanoes. I stumbled over overturned benches and smashed flowerpots. There was broken glass just about everywhere we stepped. It reminded me of an ancient vid I'd seen of a war back in the old days when there was a place called England.

The City of London looked a bit like the plaza after some Agro types called Snazzies, or something like that, bombed the guts out of it. I also remember that although the Hinglish were all but done in, they won that particular battle.

A loud boom caused us to swivel round. The Auditorium belched out smoke blocking the entrance with rubble. We saw a shape scuttle from the carnage. Santy sped to the steps and disappeared behind one of the columns. When next she came into view, she had Lilith in her grasp. Dreng bounded up the steps, tied a restraint around her puny wrists and pushed her before him.

"Where is Deogol?"

"Gone where he belongs."

"Do nay be clever wi me, filthy Agro spy."

Lilith snickered and spat on his boots. Dreng cuffed her cheek and she coughed. Santy grabbed her hair and pulled back her head. She choked.

"Tell us where Deogol is, or I will snap your neck."

"Snap away."

I thought my Santy would, for she yanked Lilith's head backwards with such force that the Carnie/Prasiebee fell to the ground leaving a clump of her hair in Santy's fingers. "Tell me or I will stomp upon your throat." I'd never seen such a look of hatred in my Santy's eyes. She raised her foot and hovered it over Lilith's neck. "Speak now."

"Or what? You will kill me? How will that help?"

Santy lowered her boot and dragged Lilith to her feet by her tethered wrists.

"He is gone far, far away by now. Truly, I do not know where. All I did was take him from the oldie place and bring him here. A hooded male snatched him from me and told me to leave quick. I did."

"Who took him? Carnie or Agro?"

Lilith shrugged. "No idea."

My shoulders began to shake. Santy took my arms, pulled me close against her chest. When I was finished blubbing, I sniffed and stood tall. "So, what now? The entrance is blocked, so we cannot get in to search for Deogol. He is lost."

Santy blinked slowly. "No, not lost, just gone temporarily." She clenched her fingers and turned to Lilith. "What do you know?"

"Nothing more. My part in all this is

done."

"Do ye think we should take her to the fence and let the border guards interrogate her?" Dreng said.

"I do. It is good that we have found this Agro spy. I believe she knows more than she tells. Let us go quickly. We can do no more until we have a lead. Do not pout Addy, where would we look?"

Without further comment, Dreng grabbed Lilith and we walked to the perimeter fences. Then, far into the distance, past the infoplace, out towards the other part of town, I saw specks of folk coming into view. They shimmered in the hazy light like the echoes of those that had moved on. Dreng stopped. "What spookiness is this?"

"Ghosties of those you killed. God has sent them down to administer vengeance."

"Trap shut Praisebee," he said and administered a wallop across her grime-matted head.

The shapes became bigger, less obscure. They were Cityfolk from the opposite end of town. They shuffled slowly along, carrying wounded, bubs and bits and bobs of belongings. I saw a young 'un with a white tunic attached to a long slim piece of metal, walk in front. He wafted the makeshift flag to and fro before him. He shouted in a hoarse voice, "We surrender. We surrender."

I spat on the ground. "Huff me! Measly feeblebellied excuses for hominids. Giving in to the enemy just like that."

"Do not be so harsh Adara, this scuffle is unlike anything they have experienced."

"True enough. The worst things they've experienced since today is a wastebin not being emptied on time. Still, it galls me to see such cowardice."

"Only what I'd expect from the likes of you Cityfolk. With your cleaner than clean places, and your screeching at dirt and germs. If I was free I'd go around sneezing in your unsoiled faces and give you all the flu bug."

"What? You have the flu? But that damn virus was eradicated more than a hundred orbits ago wasn't it?"

"Relax Addy, Lilith doesn't have a bug, she's trying to upset you."

"Goodly job done well."

Lilith cackled.

Santy held her hands up and approached the folk. "We are not Agros, as you can see. So there is no need to brandish the sign of capitulation."

The kiddle frowned, lowered his flag and

all stopped. A fem pushing a tot in a blue stroller came forward. She was dressed in fancy duds as if on her way to a shindig. In fact as I looked around at the other folk, I realised they were all wearing their finest outfits. Oddly indeed.

"Thanks be to the OneGreatProvider. We observed and heard the skirmish in the centre square. When all the lights went out we did not know what to do. It was indeed lucky we were all attending a comingout day celebration." She looked down fondly at the bub in the shovechair. "His actually. We stayed put waiting for info, but none came. Well, we would have remained till some news arrived, but the grub is running low and the bogflushes have stopped working, so we simply had to come out."

Santy chewed her bottom lip. "We cannot bring so many to Goldenagehomes, there is not the space to house them. Were you bombed from your homes?"

"No, like I said we ran out of stuff we needed."

"The main plaza is a wreck, devastated. The homedwellings on that side of town, uninhabitable also. The residents are holed up at the oldie centre. It is stuffed to capacity. I must suggest that you all go to your own dwellings and remain there. I promise, it will not be for too long. Help is on the way."

"But, the loos, the food?"

"Search your storecupboards. There must some provisions left. Then share. As for flushings, well I can only suggest that holes be dug outside and you plop in there."

One great, "Yeuk" rang out from one and all.

The fem, face all screwed up, said, "But, but, but…" then turned to the rest. "What to do?"

They scratched their heads, opened their mouths, but no one spoke.

"Do as I suggest. You really are best at home than out there where all is chaos. All is filth."

The dazed folk did not move. They stared at Santy with a look of hopelessness. She sighed.

"Would you feel more secure if a S.A.N.T. or two accompanied you?"

"Oh yes," the mam fem said.

"Addy, the perimeter fence is not far. Are you able to take Lilith to it?"

"Most def," I said and grabbed her from Dreng. She growled. I tightened her tethers to shut her up.

"Oh let's go. At least we can remain unsullied from the dust and dirt." The ma turned around, gave us a look as if to suggest that we could do with a wash and said, "This Agro thing is most irritating."

"That it is," Santy said. She touched my shoulder. "When you have deposited that scum, go straight back to Goldenagehomes. There is not much we can do without info. I will be quick."

I nodded.

"Come, Dreng, let us deposit these frightened folk."

All turned around and walked away.

"Right, Praisebee/Carnie, move."

Lilith did and we marched to the north border fences. I was puzzled as to why the Praisebee said nowt, what with her being so vocal all other times. "What do you know of the Agro onslaught?"

"Not a thing."

"Liar."

"Perhaps, but I will not spill. Not to you."

"Yeah, well, it is of no matter. We have won the battle and you and yours have lost. We will find Deogol."

Lilith let out a great guffaw. "Believe what you will. Know this, though, amongst the rubble and here and there, I planted boom things to terrify and scare."

"What do you mean?"

"Oh, this and that. Nice little Meek, your bro."

She chortled again.

I let the back of my hand make contact with her cheek and she stopped laughing.

We arrived at the fence without further discourse. I saw many S.A.N.T.S. gathered at the guard huts. I waved to them. "Hey, hey, prisoner here. A Praisebee in cahoots with the mayor. Santy sent me. She took my bro. We need her to spill about his whereabouts," I said and prodded her. She stumbled, but was stopped from falling by a border guard. He took her by the restraint and pulled her towards the hut. He pushed her inside the wooden cabin and before he closed the door I saw S.A.N.T.S. and guards swarm around Lilith like flies on a dead thing.

I caught her eye. She snorted and shouted out, "I will be rewarded for what I have done. They will come for me. I gave them something special." A guard thwacked her. She fell to the floor.

Turning to the guard that remained outside, I said, "What will they do with her?"

"Interrogate and find out what she knows."

"What, all of them?"

"She may be more willing to give out when encompassed by so many of the enemy."

"Goodly plan."

"We have word that Carnies disguised as Agros may yet arrive, we must be well informed of their strategy. She knows what is what."

Although I was fearful for my bro, I did not think that more scuffles were to come.

"But, I thought the battle won?"

He raised an eyebrow by way of response.

## Chapter Twenty-Six
*More Bangs And Booms*

My journey back to Goldenagehome should have been quick, but the words that Lilith said about devices and boomings, played upon my mind like a kiddle on a swingbar. I changed my direction and headed back to Centralplaza.

All was still and quiet, except for a wind that swished around the buildings. I looked to where Santy and Dreng had gone with the other folk. There came a gut-churning explosion. A great plume of smoke appeared from the far end of town. Two more bangs, more smoke, then the sound of many cries and wailings.

I raced towards the noise and saw many folk stumble from their dwellings, crying, cut, and bloody. I ran amongst them asking where Santy and Dreng were, but they did not respond. So I shouted loud and frequent until my throat closed over.

More dust and blood-covered residents emerged. They staggered past me as I tried to make my way to a building, not unlike Puritytowers, only smaller. All the glass was gone. Not a pane remained. It looked like a massive metal skeleton. Folk tumbled out from the vast smashed-in doorways. Behind them, I saw Dreng carrying Santy. I legged it quick. "Santy! Santy!"

"Hush now lassie, hush. She is broken and needs help. As do the others."

Santy twitched her lids. "Santy it's me, Adara."

"Put me down."

Dreng gently lowered her to the floor. I knelt beside her.

"Are you badly injured?"

"Might be this time, but help me to stand and let us go back to your Grangran, where it is safe. The others must come too."

We helped her to her feet and between us we half carried, half dragged her towards Goldenagehomes. We paused. I shouted to the stumbling folk, "Follow us to a safe place. Please, do not dawdle, or question, just follow and quickly." Without waiting for a reply, we walked on.

"Ye have a voice of authority upon ye. See how eagerly they tramp behind us without question?"

Indeed, they did march behind. It took a longly time to get to Goldenagehomes. Orva was astounded when she opened the gate and saw the many wounded we brought with us. "Ah, Breanna, no," she said and called over to a S.A.N.T. guard. He and Dreng supported Santy. She was out of it.

Her head was slumped against her chest, her left arm hung down as if all the bones had been removed. Blood soaked her right trouser leg and it took all of my self-control not to fling my arms around her. They carried her away and Orva touched my arm. "All these folk, what occurred? I heard a distant booming and was anxious."

"We found Lilith, but not Deogol. She was planting bombs as it turned out. She is with the border guards now."

Orva winced and then looked over my shoulder at the straggly bombed-out residents. "There must be near a hundred folk. Not too badly damaged by the looks of things. Bring them in."

I beckoned to the sad-faced, they limped behind me and we went inside. I moved folk out of the way so that the injured could be laid down. The floor was hard and cold. I could not bring myself to let these casualties that included bubs, to sit upon it.

I looked around the room for something to use as cushions. I was raging inside thinking about Deogol's safety and when I saw Drysi standing in the corner surrounded by her bags, I marched over. "Got anything we could use to put on the ground so those that are sick do not have to feel the coldness of the stone beneath them?"

"Nope. All this stuff is mine. I won't have it sullied by blood and filth."

Grabbing a large carryall that was propped against the wall, I turned to leave, but was prevented from doing so. I felt my hair being pulled and swung the bag around. It caught Drysi in the stomach. She crumpled to the floor gasping for breath. Her ma and da fluttered round her like ants on some sweetie crumbs.

I left them to it. Opening the bag, I pulled out skirts, tunics and some softly blankies, then placed them on the ground. "You must rest where you can." They did and I went in search of my Greatgrangran.

She sat alone by the window. I waved. She looked past me and said, "Have you seen Deogol? He said he needed a plop and went to the poop room."

"He is gone."

"Where?"

"Don't know. Wish I did, though. The fem Praisebee took him."

"Where to?"

"Lilith won't say, not yet anyway."

"He must be found. You must search for him and bring him back."

"Duh, I know!" I shouted too loudly for tears gathered at Grangran's eyes. I wrapped my arms around her and together we let out our grief in stuttering gasps.

"Santy is badly injured too."

Grangran let me go. "How bad?"

I did not answer.

"I must go to her. Bad enough when I lost your sweet ma and before her, your granma. I don't think I could bear to lose another of mine before I succumb to the loss of life."

"Don't take on so, Grangran. Santy is in the Medicentre. We'll go together, eh?"

She nodded and with her hand in mine we walked as quickly as her aged legs would let us to the healing place.

Once inside I clocked a nursey standing by a table in front of the rows and rows of beds all shielded by sky blue drapes. I could not see my Santy through them. "Where is Breanna?" I said.

The nursey pointed at a cubicle at the back of the room. "Last one on the right. Oh hello Amranwen, are you well?"

"Yes, yes, yes, I've come to see my young 'un," Grangran said and trundled off quicker than a beetle exposed from underneath a rock. I legged it after her and we stopped by the closed curtains of Santy's cubical.

I paused, then opened the hangings. How ill she looked. All scratched, with her face swelled up on one side. I placed my hand on her forehead. It was clammy. Grangran pushed me aside, I backed out, thinking it best to let her have time with her own granbub.

I stood a little away by another cubical, closed my eyes and heard a faint tune coming from said place. Opening my lids, I slid my hands between the drapes and peeked inside.

Elijah was sitting on the bed humming softly. He smiled and opened his mouth to let me hear the song in full. I do not know why, but the tune he sang soothed me. He stood, took my fingers, and led me to Santy.

"Can I, may I, pray for your loved one?"

I nodded, so too did Grangran. He knelt beside her bed, then sang again. It was a sweet melody, full of long notes that made me think of summer evenings, of my ma and da, before they died. I listened for a few secs then joined in.

When the air was filled with our sweet melody, as one, we ceased. Elijah stood, put his fingers to his forehead, chest and either shoulder, then said, "Lord protect this woman and keep her from harm. Bathe her in your glorious light and make her whole once more."

I thought the words quite pretty, although some I did not get the meaning of straight away. He closed his eyes did the finger thingy stuff again, then stared at Santy's face. It twitched.

"Santy? Santy, can you hear me?"

"Addy?"

"Yep, me."

Her eyes parted just enough for her to recognise my gob. I touched her cheek and she said, "Ow."

"Praisethelord," Elijah said and at that moment in time, I did too.

Leaning in close to my Santy, I put my hand on hers. She blinked and said all woozy-like, "Deogol is gone? I did not dream it?"

"Nope, you did not. Yep, he is took."

She tried to lift herself but could not. She bit her lip with the effort then sank back.

"Ah, Breanna," Grangran said and stroked her cheek. "My little Dustcloud."

Santy flinched.

Grangran turned away. "Find him. Find Deogol."

"Gladly, if I knew where I was to look."

With a huge effort, Santy raised herself. Then to my amazement, Elijah sat on the bed, supporting her whilst she spoke. "It must be that Agros have him. You must go to them. Bring him back."

"Again, gladly, if I knew where to look."

Santy squinted. "Dreng has told me that the City is on high alert after these last skirmishes. None shall enter or leave."

"But Deogol must be found."

"Indeed, he must and soon. We do not know for sure what has become of him, but there are rumours and guesses enough for a trail of sorts to be followed."

"Then I will go. There is talk of more raids to come, all guards and S.A.N.T.S. are needed here to protect folk."

"Are you ready do you think?"

"I am Santy."

Elijah shook his head. "They will not let you leave. Too much at stake. I heard them talking."

"Don't care. I need to find Deogol. No one shall stop me."

"That's my brave Addy."

Elijah furrowed his brow. "Well, if you are to go I may be able to help."

"Spill."

"I know a thing or two about entering and exiting without being noticed."

"That you do Praisebee. Give more info."

Elijah carefully let Santy's head rest on the pillow and stood. "A diversion must be put into place."

"Like what?"

"Go with your grangran."

"But I must find Deogol, how will that help?"

"I believe she is resourceful. If they will not let you out, then she may be of use in creating a diversion."

"Oh, I can do that all right," Grangran said and tapped her nose.

Santy smiled, then frowned in pain. "Go on young Praisebee, you have more to tell."

"I have info about outside that may help Adara."

"About those that abide there?"

"Yes, and beyond. We used it to skirt the dangers when sent to, to storm your city." Elijah looked around to make sure no one was looking, then hoisted up his tunic. Around his sunken chest was a bandage-like thing and I thought that he had a wound, but he did not. He quickly unwound the cloth and laid it on the bed.

In the middle was a disc sewn onto the

fabric. He unpicked a stitch or two, and pulled it free. "Here, take this," he said and handed it to me. "Try to memorise all you can. Once in the Wilderness, you must stay in the thick of it. Wolfies abide, also other folk that may try to harm you. Folk that live by instinct and are ruled by their senses. You know, hormones and stuff."

"Indeed. Wise words, young Praisebee. Addy," Santy said and beckoned for me to lean close. "Be invisible like your Synthbag. Find your bro. Gain more knowledge from what he has given you. I will send forth a message that may help. Be on your guard at all times." She squeezed my hand.

"No need to fret Santy. I will find Deogol and bring him back."

"I know you will." She let go and a nursey nudged me out of the way.

"You must leave now. Now. Let us tend to your kin."

"Fine," I said, took Greatgrangran's hand and together we walked away.

"May I come too?" Elijah said.

"Suppose, mebbe."

"Please?" He gave me a look that sent a churn throughout my gut. At once sad and terrifying, it left me quite out of sorts. I had to look away before I succumbed to a sissy leg tremble. Ah. I felt a violent moonpull twinge. The reddiness was pulsing nastily. I needed to change my sponge. "Wait for me by the exit, I need to ablush," I said and dived through the door with the stick figure fem on it.

Once inside I let loose my bowels. Then I removed my blood-soaked swab and replaced it with a fresh one. The sanity bins were not working. Neither was the hygiene spray, so I just opened the throwaway box and shoved my soiled stuff in. Water flowed though so I was able to wash. I looked at my reflection in the mirror above the sink. An older, wearier face looked back.

## Chapter Twenty-Seven
*A Diversiona*

I met Grangran and Elijah by the way-out door. Neither was talking and I sensed an aura of tense about them. With a, "Let's go," we left the Medicentre and headed back to the communal room.

Elijah sighed three times, causing me to wonder more about his part in all of this. "What happened in the tunnels Elijah?" He looked to the floor. "How did you escape?"

"I am no Agro. I was caught up in the frenzy below that is all."

I took a deeply breath not knowing for sure whether he could be trusted.

We continued our tramp back to the main quarter in silence.

When we arrived, the place was full of weary looking folk. They sat, or stood as if rocks had been placed upon their shoulders. All slumped or sagged. All gave off a vibe of gloom.

Even Meilyr looked down of face as he went amongst them offering kind words and bits of grub. He was a gentle, resourceful, kind, attentive male. Yep, a goodly sort for sure. What? Meilyr? Nah! Utter foolishness. I turned from him with a deep-lung sigh and shrugged off my pash thoughts towards the nursey male. I spied Orva chatting to one of the injured and waved to her.

Greatgrangran tutted. "Get me when you are ready. That oldie gent knows a thing or two. I'll have a confab with him. The gate was opened, that is fact. I will find out who is responsible." She wandered off to sit with said oldie male at the far side of the room.

"Good meet with your Santy?" Orva said.

"Yep. She will be well. I am to find my bro, since you all are needed here. But with the place being on lockdown, it might prove a problem. Elijah gave me this," I showed her the infodisc.

She flared her nostrils and looked at him. "Did he now? Come, you can play it on my portacomp," she said and led us to the back of the place, where it was less crowded. She gave a stern look to the bods that sat at a table, they left swiftly.

We sat, she pulled out a small compdevice from her leg pouch, and slipped in the disc. I watched image after image of the place called the Wilderness.

"Wow. That's where the Woodsfolk live?"

"Yep. And the Wolfies, and other folk,"

Elijah said.

"Other?"

"Not a threat."

"Woodsfolk are?"

"They have their own ways, best to keep clear. Best to be vigilant in case Carnies roam too."

I gulped. Orva touched my hand. "Do not be too a-feared. I have seen how you handle yourself when danger is present. You know, you are strong and fearless, you will prevail. Besides, there are always those who are amongst the brush and bramble to assist."

"Hope so. Hope I can save my bro."

"You will."

Elijah scratched his thin red hair, looked at something that stuck in his fingernail and said, "What will happen to Lilith?"

"If she survives the interrogation and gives out the info we need, she will be held with the other Agro prisoners."

"She is no Agro."

"Well, she is now. The sec she decided to side with them."

He could not make eye contact with me and fidgeted with his wide belt. I leant close to him. Orva narrowed her eyes. Elijah's pale skin became whiter.

"Maybe you need to be interrogated. We

are moving all the prisoners to the Decontamination Place. It is solid and will make a goodly jail for them until we decide what is best for their future."

Touching Elijah on the arm, I said all low-like, "Spill now. You do not want to go to that building, not for all the seeds in what is left of this land."

Elijah blinked slowly and wiped his face with both hands. Orva folded her arms and gave him a dark look that made me shiver.

"Lilith had a device. I caught her talking to someone on it. She hit me hard. When I woke, Agros, or Carnies, or whoever they are, were there laying explosives. She was eating cake and choc, taunting me with the delicacies. She told them to leave me, then left. Everything went boom. I ran after them dodging bangs and bits of rubble. When we got to the outside, I caught up with her. She didn't say anything. We fled here. She kept mumbling things about the mayor and how when we were safe she would do such dreadful things to me if I blabbed, that I swore I would not tell of her part in planning the Praisebee diversion with the mayor. That is it, that is all."

"That is enough," Orva said. "You will be treated well. Better than the other prisoners.

You will come with me."

"What? No, Orva, you cannot take him to the Decontamination place, you cannot. He gave me the disc, he has been of help." I stood in front of the trembling Praisebee.

"Please, Adara, do not concern yourself with these matters. He will be treated well enough. He is not a threat, but, he was with Lilith. He knows more than he remembers."

Elijah looked to me, but I could do nowt except shrug. He did the finger to head and shoulder thingy again.

Orva called to Dreng. "Take him with the others. He has been helpful and will be again, no doubt. He will be not so much a prisoner, as an informer. Accommodate him accordingly."

"Dreng, wait a sec," I said and indicated that he follow me to a distance away from the others. When far enough away so as not to be heard, I said, "He is not a threat, he is good. Treat him well, you can see that he has suffered."

"Aye, that is clear. Ye need not concern yerself for his well-being lassie."

"But still. He is an innocent."

Dreng twisted his mouth and rubbed his chin. "Perhaps. I will see to it myself that he comes to nay harm. It is all I can do. Try to focus on yer mission, not the fate of one who is caught up in something wrong."

"You are right. You are Woodsfolk are you not?"

"Aye, that I am."

"What must I fear from them?"

His eyes opened wide. "Nowt. We are peaceful and friendly. Oh wait, except, stay clear of the Nearly camp. It is deep into the woods, ye should have nay cause to wander that far in."

"Right. Elijah said some stuff about them that I didn't quite glean."

"Ye will if ye meet them."

"I shall endeavour not to do so then."

Orva came over to us and made a head tilt in the direction of Elijah. Dreng nodded, walked over to him and put his hand on his back.

Elijah looked at me with fear.

Although it was hard to meet his gaze, I gave him what I hoped was an encouraging smile, before Dreng touched his elbow and guided him to the Foodpreproom where the other fake Agros remained.

"Are you ready to leave, Adara?"

I sucked in then let out a deeply sigh. "As good as I 'spose, Orva."

"You have supplies and the like?"

"Yep. All in my Synthbag."

"Here," she said and took some oval brown things from her trouser leg pouch. "Vombombs. Throw one of these on a bod and they'll chuck up their guts till nowt is left but air."

I took the grenades from her and put them into my Synthbag. "Do you think we should wait until nightfall?"

"Do you wish to?"

"Nah, nope, best get going before I get a bout of wobbleg and change my mind."

"You know, Adara, your Santy would not send you unless you were able."

"Yeah, I know. I guess." Looking around the room, I saw Grangran still chitchatting with the oldie male. I waved to her, she waved back.

Orva shook her head and then pushed me towards my grangran. "Give her a proper byebye, Adara."

I went to her and she took my hands in her wrinkly ones. She smiled as though I were about to go to the park for a game of footsieball rather than a deadly mission. But I was glad for that, for my insides whirled around like the falling seedpods from a sycamore tree.

She brushed hair away from my face and

patted my cheek. "Ah, now. Not so good at the leavetaking stuff. I'll go with you to the border and create a distraction whilst you slip over the fence. Give me something to do eh?"

"Ta Grangran."

The oldie male she had been talking to, which I recognised as being one of the 'dults that used their stick as barriers, handed his cane to her. "Here Amranwen, in case things get nasty." She took the weapon from him and together we walked to the exit.

Meilyr followed. He touched my arm. "I heard you are to leave. Be careful," he said and slipped a bar of Sterichoc into my hand.

I came over all girlygig for a sec and embraced him most fondly. He blushed then returned to the communal room.

"He's a goodun'. Make someone a goodly hubby," Grangran said and winked.

Thankfully Orva arrived and any more talk of Meilyr or hints of joining with said male vanished. "Ready?"

"Ready."

We squared our shoulders, stood tall and left the safety of Goldenagehomes to make our way to the South perimeter fence.

Linking my Grangran, I said, "Did you find out who opened the gate?"

"There is a suspect."

"Who?"

"Deogol."

"Wa? No."

"He was seen. Identified. Think on, Adara. We don't know what he was up to on the comps, but whatever it was, it made him turn against his own. I am not sure if he is right of mind, I truly don't." She stared at me for a sec, all serious-like and said, "Folk are devious. Trust no one."

I could not believe my bro would do such a thing unless greatly coerced. So much turmoil and sadness had occurred of late. No wonder he became confused and afraid.

Perhaps he was told of safety.

Perhaps lured out by promises of keeping us all unharmed.

Perhaps, perhaps, perhaps.

My noggin swirled. I shook my head to dispel the nasty thoughts that began to take shape against my bro. No, he was the victim. He was took against his will. I knew that. I knew that he must be found and brought back. With a wipe of my nose, I gulped and squeezed Grangran's hand.

We walked slowly so as not to tire her, although, to her credit, she trod quite nimbly for one of her advancing years. I looked towards Centralplaza and saw S.A.N.T.S. and Minion trucks swarm towards it, and hoped that soon all would be restored.

The ground became less even the further away from the hub of things we went. Orva took Greatrangran's arm and helped her manage the rough trail we walked along. I felt rocks and small stones under my feet. They made far more contact with my flesh than I would have liked, and I began to wish that I had been able to change my footwear from fashionable to practical.

The perimeter fence came into view. It was higher than I remembered and spiky at the top. Although I could easily climb the wire-stringed structure, I was concerned that it may be switched on to full capacity.

"Orva, is the fence alive?"

"Don't know for sure. Wouldn't think so, what with the power going off. Don't fret Adara. I have a negatekey and will use that to nullify the barrier, just in case."

Orva leant close to Greatgrangran and whispered something into her ear. Grangran giggled, put the walking stick in front of her, and leant hard upon it. She feigned feebleness so well that I almost went to her aid. She staggered up to the guard hut and all but fell into the arms of the 'dults on duty.

Orva pushed me out of eye view and said all low, "When you see me enter then leave the guard hut, climb over the fence. Run faster than you have before. Then go into the shrubbery. Wait a few secs, and continue."

"What then?"

"All will be revealed as you journey. Apparently, things are in play."

"They are?"

"Yep. Ready?"

"Nope. Yep. Yeah, ready."

With a grin, Orva gave me a hearty slap on the arm, then marched over to where Greatgrangran was wheezing and moaning. Orva slow-blinked and my Grangran grabbed onto one of the guards so hard that she almost dragged him to the ground.

She feigned more coughs and shortness of breath. He leant close and tapped her back, totally engrossed in her condition. Orva took the other guard by the arm and went into the hut. A few secs later they came out.

My cue to climb the fence.

Picking up a stone, I threw it onto the structure. It did not trigger the alarm, so I guessed it had no power. I took one lastly look back, then placed my hands and feet upon the bendy wire strands.

Taking in a deeply breath, I climbed up and over the fence.

Once on the other side, I rushed into some dense shrubbery and knelt down. I parted some large-leafed greenly thing and saw Greatgrangran tugging on the coat lapels of the guard. She pulled and pummelled him out of sight.

I wished I could have told her how brave she was.

I was about to leave when Orva and the other guard came up to the fence, just where I was hiding. She turned her back on me and leant all casual-like against the barrier, whilst the guard threw something over it. It landed behind me. I picked up a knotted piece of cloth.

Opening it, I saw a hastily drawn map showing squiggles that looked like a path through the trees before me. Then I heard the guard say in a quiet voice, "You who have taken flight to who knows where or why, might consider making your way towards the end of the forest before you. Easy to do if you keep the sun on your right shoulder and look to the map from time to time. More will be revealed when you do."

He swivelled round and both he and Orva strode away.

I waited for them to join Greatgrangran, and whilst all three were busy attempting to restrain her, I crawled slowly away.

Then stopped 'bruptly.

There came a sound in my noggin, like a voice whispering to me.

Or was it just the wind rustling the blades of grass.

I sniffed, lifted my head and breathed in the mulchy scent of the wild outdoors.

The Wilderness called to me.

I answered from my gut with a raw, shrill warble that burned my throat.

Then I hunkered low and crawled away from Cityplace to find my bro.

## The End

Nicola McDonagh

Thank you for reading my book.
If you enjoyed *Whisper Gatherers*, I would be so grateful if you could find the time to leave a review.
US: http://amzn.to/216H92W
UK: http://amzn.to/1OjRXXG
Many thanks.

Nicola McDonagh


You can purchase all three books in the series on Amazon:
US http://amzn.to/1pF2YuQ
UK http://amzn.to/1OjRXXG

Continue the gripping story with
**Echoes from the Lost Ones**
Book 2 in The Song of Forgetfulness series.
http://www.amazon.com/dp/B00YPH91E0

**The struggle to survive just got harder.**

After Agros abduct her brother, Adara leaves Cityplace and embarks on a perilous quest to find Deogol through the ravaged, terrain of NotSoGreatBritAlbion.

# FREE DOWNLOAD

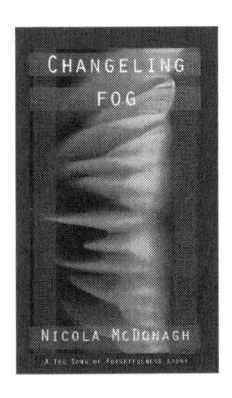

## Exclusive new story from The Song of Forgetfulness

*Carnies - Cannibal renegades have come to Cityplace. With them a clinging fog that makes the gentle occupants turn into savage beasts.*

Sign up to the author's mailing list to download this FREE short story. Plus - get news about giveaways, more free downloads, and new releases.

To receive your FREE short story 'Changeling Fog' just click on the link at:
http://www.thesongofforgetfulness.com

## Nicola McDonagh

Nicola McDonagh was born in Liverpool, the youngest of six children. She grew up amidst books, music and lots of animals. She originally trained as a photojournalist, but her love of the theatre and story telling, saw her gaining an Honours Degree in Drama and English Literature. She spent many years as an actor, scriptwriter and workshop leader, but gave it up to concentrate on her writing. She is a creative writing/photography tutor, and editor.

Nicola gained a Diploma in Creative Writing from the UEA, won the Suffolk Book League's Short Story Competition, and was shortlisted for The Escalator Genre Fiction Competition. The following year her debut novel, *Echoes from the Lost Ones,* book 2 in the series, *The Song of Forgetfulness,* was published by Fable Press. However, the series has been re-vamped and Nicola has self-published all the books so far in the series.

Follow her on:

| | |
|---|---|
| Facebook: | www.facebook.com/thesongofforgetfulness |
| Twitter: | @McDonaghNikki |
| Blog page: | www.nicolajmcdonagh.wordpress.com |
| Websites: | www.thesongofforgetfulness.com |

## What people are saying about Whisper Gatherers, Echoes from the Lost Ones and A Silence Heard

**Whisper Gatherers:**

"If you like action, and science fiction then you'll appreciate one of the first books EVER that gives you high powered adrenalin with chilling revelations of utter suspense! This book is amazing to read and you will not want to put it down!"

"The author does a great job of drawing you in with her futuristic descriptions, at times it felt like I was watching a movie, that's how enthralled I was with the book."

"The central character has a convincing mixture of wilfulness and self-deprecation, and the imagined world is sufficiently complex to provoke thought and wonder. Nice to know that there are further episodes to pursue. A good read."

"There's danger, humour, pathos, and lots of fast-paced action that makes this book a very exciting read."

**Echoes from the Lost Ones:**

There is a lot going on in this book set in a dark dystopian future, but the characters are brilliant, real, and quirky, and keep everything moving along nicely. I loved the unique language, and both the style and the voice of the book reminded me of Patrick Ness' Walking Chaos Trilogy. I would definitely recommend it to people who enjoy his books! A brilliant and unique read for adults and young adults alike. Very impressed and will be reading the next instalment."

"Addictive and engrossing-. It creates its own unique world where there's danger, and fear, and regret, but where there is a barrel load of humour, too…"

"A great story full of fun wordplay, great imagery, and an underlying commentary about the frailties of mankind."

"A story of trust and faith "Echoes from the Lost Ones" is an adventure that takes you to a time and place like no other."

"Post apocalyptic world where people worry about when they're next going to be able to go to the loo! Genius, why did no one write this before."

**A Silence Heard:**

"A Silence Heard was action oriented and perilous! I was definitely on the edge of my seat as I read, waiting to find out what happened next!'

'A world in which morals do not exist and yet somehow this little band manage to maintain a sense of compassion and humanity. It is a fight for survival against a cruel and destructive enemy who tries to obliterate any good left on the earth. Tremendous read for young adults who I'm sure will identify with the futuristic genre of the book."

"I admire that the author had the courage to set the personal stakes for Adara very high in this volume. War is a messy business, and it comes at a horrific cost. That's a tough lesson and one that many authors gloss over for fear of alienating readers. Heroes have to win some and lose some, or the story becomes implausible and lacks tension. That's certainly not the case in A Silence Heard. I look forward to the next volume."

Whisper Gatherers

Made in the USA
Charleston, SC
07 September 2016